SHOWDOWN!

"Stop, Bolt!" Laurette cried out, her voice shaky and shrill with hysteria. "Please! For my sake, don't do this thing!"

Lew Badham swaggered out onto the boardwalk in front of the saloon, his arms held away from his body, his hands close to his guns. "You gonna hide behind that French whore's skirts, Bolt?" he called.

"Badham, you're nothing but a snake," Bolt hissed. "And you have insulted a lady. Make your move!"

"First draw?"

"That's right."

Bolt watched the gunman's eyes, not his flashing hands. Badham's eyes crinkled, narrowed to slits.

Bolt knew it was the instant of truth.

BOLT IS A LOVER AND A FIGHTER!

BOLT
Zebra's Blockbuster Adult Western Series
by Cort Martin

#13: MONTANA MISTRESS	(1316, $2.25)
#17: LONE STAR STUD	(1632, $2.25)
#18: QUEEN OF HEARTS	(1726, $2.25)
#19: PALOMINO STUD	(1815, $2.25)
#20: SIX-GUNS AND SILK	(1866, $2.25)
#21: DEADLY WITHDRAWAL	(1956, $2.25)
#22: CLIMAX MOUNTAIN	(2024, $2.25)
#23: HOOK OR CROOK	(2123, $2.50)
#24: RAWHIDE JEZEBEL	(2196, $2.50)

Available wherever paperbacks are sold, or order direct from the Publisher. Send cover price plus 50¢ per copy for mailing and handling to Zebra Books, Dept. 2387, 475 Park Avenue South, New York, N.Y. 10016. Residents of New York, New Jersey and Pennsylvania must include sales tax. DO NOT SEND CASH.

BOLT #26
MAVERICK MISTRESS

CORT MARTIN

ZEBRA BOOKS
KENSINGTON PUBLISHING CORP.

ZEBRA BOOKS

are published by

Kensington Publishing Corp.
475 Park Avenue South
New York, NY 10016

Copyright © 1988 by Cort Martin

All rights reserved. No part of this book may be reproduced in any form or by any means without the prior written consent of the Publisher, excepting brief quotes used in reviews.

First printing: June, 1988

Printed in the United States of America

CHAPTER ONE

Jared Bolt reached up high and ripped the fancy flyer down from the pole at the corner of Main and Third in San Antonio. The tacks groaned and flew onto the dusty street as the pasteboard came free. Tom Penrod reached down and picked up one of the tacks, felt its sharp point.

"What's it say?" he asked, looking over Bolt's shoulder at the pen-and-ink drawing of the curvaceous woman on the poster.

"Looks like Monte Calhoun has him a new singer at the Prairie Schooner," said Bolt. "She's from New Orleans. Pretty French name."

"Laurette Armand?" Tom asked.

"Yes. Laurette Armand." Bolt repeated the name slowly as he held the flyer out at arm's length and studied the pen-and-ink drawing. "It has a nice ring to it."

"Never heard of her."

"Me neither," Bolt grinned, "but, if she looks

anything like her picture, she'll drive the fellows wild."

"Maybe Monte Calhoun has finally found a class act for the Prairie Schooner."

"Or maybe he just got lucky," Bolt said dryly. "Monte wouldn't know real talent from a bunch of baboons. I think he's already proved that."

"What's that chan-two-see down there?" Tom leaned closer to read the block letters stamped on the poster.

"A *chanteuse*. That's a fancy French word for singer."

"What about that name down there at the bottom?" Tom pointed. "I like it better than the name Laurette Armand. Easier to say."

"What? Ken Selves, pianist?" Bolt asked.

"No. Cherie Bonwit, bells," read Penrod. He said it "Cherry."

"That's Sheree, Tom," Bolt said wryly, "and if Laurette Armand looks anything like her picture, she can't be."

"Can't be what?"

"Cherry," said Bolt.

"Yeah, you're probably right," Tom laughed. "But, what the hell? Her show opens tonight. Let's go see what she's got to offer."

"Go ahead, Tom, but you'll go by yourself."

"You mean you're not going?" Tom looked at his friend in surprise.

"Nope. I don't plan to waste a whole day in town just to attend her opening at eight o'clock tonight. I got better things to do with my time." Bolt continued to stare at the pen-and-ink drawing.

"You mean, you're gonna turn down a chance to see this beautiful, sexy creature in person?"

"She is sexy, isn't she?" Bolt grinned. "But that's what I mean, Tom. I ain't settin' foot inside the Prairie Schooner." Bolt lowered the flyer.

"Well, if that don't beat all." Tom shook his head. "You surprise me, Bolt. Your curiosity usually gets the best of you."

"Not this time, Tom. I ain't gonna plunk down good money to see another one of Calhoun's circuses."

"It's only a dollar to get in," Tom said. "Any show is worth that."

"It's a dollar too much. Don't you remember that last flimflam Monte tried to pull on the public?"

"You mean when he was supposed to have beautiful, seductive sirens, straight from their island at sea? Yes, I remember." Tom laughed. "They turned out to be horse-faced dogs, every damned one of them."

"That's what I'm talking about, Tom. Remember the flyers? And the drawing of four, pretty, bare-breasted nymphs cavorting about the rocks? Calhoun billed them as a bevy of beautiful sirens who would seduce the men with their sweet songs."

"Well, you gotta admit, Calhoun packed the place with that little ruse."

"Yeah, for one performance, until the customers realized they'd been duped. Monte Calhoun uses cheap gimmicks to attract the hardy fools to his saloon."

"Including us, Bolt."

"That's right, Tom. It worked before, but I learned my lesson. I have no doubts but what this is another one of Monte's cheap tricks," Bolt said as he tapped the pen-and-ink drawing with his index finger, "and this time, I don't want to be counted among the fools who fall for it."

"You really don't like Monte Calhoun, do you?"

"No, and I'm sure the feeling is mutual," Bolt said. "He's jealous because we run a bordello out at our ranch. After all, Monte bought the Prairie Schooner to turn it into a whorehouse."

"I know," said Tom, "and the Women's Church Society kicked up their heels and put a stop to it."

"That's when Calhoun resorted to his cheap tricks to make a go of the saloon. But I don't know why he resents me. Hell, it ain't my fault he's a failure. If he had just played it straight, he'd have the most popular saloon in San Antonio by now."

Tom looked at the poster again and shook his head. "Well, she sure is pretty," he said with a big sigh.

"Quit your drooling, Tom. There ain't no gal as beautiful as the one on this here flyer. And even if there was, do you think she'd be at Calhoun's place? Use your head for something other than a hat rack."

"It'd be worth the price to find out, wouldn't it?" Tom said with a lustful grin.

"Hey, Tom, if you want to see Miss Armand, go ahead and go. Join the rest of the fools. Then you can tell me all about it and we can both have a good laugh."

"I think I'll just do that, Bolt." He stretched his neck to look at the drawing of the singer again. "She's so damned purty."

At that moment, they heard a man yell and both men turned to look up the street. The boardwalk rattled as a small, thin man, wearing a derby hat and dressed in a gray broadcloth suit, scrambled away from a large, burly man carrying a packet of posters under one huge arm and a tack hammer in his other hand.

"Look out," yelled Tom, as the smaller man launched himself from the boardwalk onto the street, racing in their direction.

"Stop, you little weasel," ordered the bigger man.

"Help me!" screeched the thin man, heading straight for Bolt.

Tom stepped to one side. Bolt tried to get out of the way, but the small man, his face contorted in terror, adjusted his course and dashed straight at Bolt, knocking the poster from Bolt's hands.

Bolt reared back, struggling to maintain his balance. The big man, faster than he looked, jumped from the boardwalk, grabbed the small man by his coat collar and jerked him backward, knocking the derby from his head. The tack hammer jutted out of the giant man's clenched fist, the one that had the little man's coat bunched up in it like a hank of rag.

"Hold on there," said Bolt as the big man snatched the small man away.

"Out of my way," said the big man. He tucked the tack hammer in his wide belt and drew back a hammy fist, aiming it at the little man's jaw.

Bolt's hand shot out, grabbed the big man's wrist. The little man squirmed like a skewered worm.

"Drop him," said Bolt, cocking a fist of his own.

"Christ, Bolt," said Tom, "this is none of our business."

The big man glowered and released the small man, who dropped to the ground like a sack of meal, landing square on his derby hat. The barrel-chested man dropped his posters, as well, and smashed Bolt's arm away. Then he waded into Bolt, both fists flailing like scythes. Bolt took a blow high on his cheekbone and staggered backwards, lights dancing in his skull. The giant lurched forward, pressing his advantage. Tom swung and missed as the big man passed him, ignoring Penrod in his pursuit of Bolt.

While the others weren't looking, the small man cowering on the ground retrieved his flattened derby hat, which was now covered with dust and dirt. He slowly crawled away from the melee on his hands and knees, pulling his head and neck down into his shoulders like a turtle. When he was half a block away, he glanced back over his shoulder at the brawling men, then quickly stood up and ran on up the street as fast as his short legs would carry him.

"You sonofabitch," said the big man and he threw a massive left square at Bolt's jaw. Bolt ducked under it and went into a fighting crouch. He sidestepped, and rammed a fist into the big man's belly, burying it to the wrist. The blow didn't even faze the big man, who still had his hat in place. He cornered and came back with a roundhouse right that had steam behind it.

The blow caught Bolt in the chest, staggered him off-balance, jolting him to his socks.

A couple of passersby stopped to watch, but kept their distance.

The big brute clenched his ham-hock fist, drew back, prepared to follow through on his advantage before Bolt could regain his balance. Tom grabbed the attacker's crooked arm from behind, jerking it back with a brutal, twisting motion.

The big man grunted with pain and spun around, shook his thick arm free from Tom's clutches. He drew back again, this time aiming a punch at Penrod's face.

Tom stuck out his left arm to ward off the attack and caught the brunt of the blow in his upper arm as hard knuckles crunched into his flesh. Ignoring the pain that seared through his brain, Tom swung with a right punch that smashed into the big man's jaw. The jolting impact of the blow snapped the fellow's head back and sent his hat sailing off his head. The huge brute of a man sported a thick moustache and a dark, bushy beard, but had only fringes of dark hair around his bald pate.

The fight moved up onto the boardwalk and four men emerged from the nearby mercantile store. They didn't venture more than a few feet away from the doorway as they stood and watched the fisticuffs. Two primly dressed women watched the brawling men from inside, the expression on their faces full of curiosity behind the smudgy window of the mercantile shop.

The giant's head jerked back momentarily, but he

came back with both fists swinging like monstrous clubs.

Tom was ready for him and got in two quick jabs to the man's chin before he caught a glancing blow across his own cheek. Tom stumbled sideways, ducked out of the way of a forceful punch.

Bolt jumped back into the fray. He swung with a powerful uppercut to the fellow's chin, then brought his knee up hard into the big, lumbering man's groin.

Cheers went up from the gathering crowd. A couple of bystanders booed the low blow.

The big man groaned in pain, dropped his hands to his crotch, lowered his head. Bolt moved in and started boxing the man's ears, both of them at the same time, as if the giant's bald head were a punching bag.

Still holding his aching crotch, the man tried to back away from Bolt's stinging attack on his ears. Bolt followed him and stopped punching the big man's ears only long enough to deliver two quick jabs to the fellow's bulbous nose.

"Stop! Stop!" the giant man cried out as he lowered his head even more. Bolt continued his assault on the fellow's oversized ears and then struck a hard blow to the top of the giant's bald head. Tom came up from the side and with the side of his open hand, he delivered two quick chops to the back of the assailant's thick neck.

Bolt jammed his fist into the man's nose. Blood spurted from both nostrils.

"Please stop," the man called again as he tried to bring one of his arms up over his ears. He wiped at his nose with the back of his other hand.

Bolt doubled up his fist.

"Stop! I give up," the big man shouted as he tucked his chin against his chest and wrapped both arms around his head.

Bolt shoved the huge fellow up against the side of the mercantile building. The two matronly women who were watching through the dirty window jumped back and disappeared from sight. Bolt stepped back and caught his breath as Tom, panting for air, came up and stood beside him.

"What in the hell was that all about?" Bolt demanded. "Why were you attacking that little runt of a fellow?"

The big man patted his nose gingerly, as if to see if it were broken. His moustache was bright red with the blood that dripped from his nose and trickled through his beard before it spilled onto his clothing, leaving crimson stains across the vast expanse of his white shirt. He was in a state of disarray with his shirttail hanging out and his clothes rumpled and dusty from the fray. With his jaw set tight, his teeth clenched stubbornly, he glowered at Bolt and refused to answer.

"What's your name, big boy?" Bolt asked.

"None of your damned business, mister," the big man answered through clenched teeth.

Bolt took a step toward the lumbering hulk. He rubbed his bruised cheekbone.

"Whenever someone takes a punch at me, I make it my business to find out his name."

"It's Clyde. Clyde Pulaski," the fellow snarled.

He put a finger under his nose where the flow of blood had slowed to an ooze.

"And why were you chasin' after that scrawny little fellow?" Bolt asked.

"You had no right to interfere," the big man said sullenly. He wiped his nose with the sleeve of his shirt.

"And if we hadn't interfered, you would have pounded him to mush."

"Why don't you pick on someone your own size, buster?" Tom said sarcastically.

"And why don't you two bastards mind your own damned business?" the big fellow said. He sniffed, trying to breathe through his clogged nose.

Disappointed that the excitement was over, the crowd began to disperse. Only two of the men near the mercantile doorway stuck around to see if the fighting would begin again.

"We were minding our own business," Bolt said, "until you and your little pip-squeak friend came crashing into us."

"He ain't a friend of mine. Where is he?" Clyde asked, his dark eyes suddenly narrowing to slits as he glanced around. He looked on the ground, then stepped away from the wall and peered up the street. "Where is that sonofabitchin' little weasel?"

Bolt shoved Pulaski back against the wall. "Forget it, big boy. You already scared the pants off that poor fellow."

"That prissy little coward," Pulaski mumbled as he pushed himself away from the wall and tucked his shirttail in. "He started this whole damned thing, trying to tell me what to do."

The two fellows at the doorway of the mercantile shop shook their heads and went back inside, satisfied that the fight was over.

"And just what did he do to make you so damned mad?" Bolt asked.

"He told me I was hangin' them flyers too high," Clyde said. "Not my fault he's such a runt."

"You did put 'em up too high," Bolt said. "I'm six foot tall and I had to stretch my neck to read the one that was tacked up on that pole over there. That's why I tore it down."

"Yeah, well, that prissy little bastard had no business tellin' me to tear down all them flyers and then tack 'em back up two feet lower. Hell, he didn't hire me to put 'em up, and he sure as hell don't have the right to tell me how to do it or where to put 'em."

"Prissy or not, a man your size doesn't go around beating up a little fellow like that just because he disagrees with you," Bolt said. "Not unless you intend to kill him."

"He pushed me into it." Clyde made another swipe at his nose with his shirt-sleeve. "I told that little, whiney voiced runt to shut up and leave me alone before I smashed his ugly face to pulp, but the little bastard kept it up."

"You mean he hit you?" Tom asked.

"No, but he sure as hell wanted to." Pulaski laughed. "He even made a puny little fist and threatened to strike me. But when he saw that he was no match for me, he grabbed my box of tacks and threw it out into the street. When I saw those tacks scattered all over the road, that's when I got hot."

"You've got a mean temper, big boy," Bolt said.

"Hell, I wasn't fixin' to hit him," Clyde whined. "I was just gonna make that puny little weasel pick up all them tacks he spilled. But when I reached for him, he run off like a scared chicken."

"Can't say as I blame him," Tom said. "You're three times his size."

"Then he shouldn't have messed with me in the first place," Pulaski said.

"So you work for Monte Calhoun," Bolt said. "It figures."

"No, I don't work for him," said Pulaski. "I was just in the Prairie Schooner this morning, nursin' a hangover and watchin' Miss Armand rehearse for tonight's opening, when the printer delivered the flyers. Monte told me he'd let me see the show free tonight and he'd also pay for all my drinks if I'd put those posters up all over town."

"Cheap labor," Tom commented.

Clyde Pulaski glanced down at the flyers that were scattered in the street, half of them dirty and ruined because they'd been trampled on during the scuffle. "Dammit, now I gotta pick up all them posters and then go back and pick up all them tacks by myself. I could strangle that little runt."

"Do you know who that little fellow is?" Bolt asked.

"The runt? Yeah, I know who he is," Clyde said with disgust. "That's the stupid little piano player Miss Armand brought with her from New Orleans. His name's Ken Selves."

"That's Ken Selves?" Tom asked.

"Yeah. I can't stand his squeaky little voice. He struts about, bossin' people around like he owns the show. Well, he ain't gonna boss me around."

Bolt turned to Tom and shook his head. "I told you, Tom. If that scrawny little fellow is Miss Armand's pianist, then I'll bet Laurette Armand is a big, fat, horse-faced opera singer."

"Oh, no, she ain't," said Pulaski before Tom could reply. "Miss Armand sings like an angel and she's the purtiest little gal I ever laid eyes on. Hell, you saw her picture on the flyer, didn't you?"

"We saw it, but we didn't believe it," Bolt said wryly. "Monte Calhoun is known for his deceptive schemes to draw customers into his saloon. The Schooner's been a losing proposition ever since he opened it and he'd do anything to make a quick buck off the suckers who fall for his tricks."

"I know," said Clyde, "but he's gonna pack 'em in with Miss Armand performing there. When I went by Ted's Barbershop a few minutes ago, the fellers were already lined up waiting to get a shave and a haircut. And a whole bunch of 'em were even waitin' in line to take a bath and it ain't even Saturday night," he chuckled. "Hell, Ted's gonna make himself a fortune today, and Monte's gonna make a bundle of bucks from now on with Laurette Armand."

"What about that other gal?" Tom asked. "Cherie Bonwit?" He still pronounced it "Cherry."

"She's a purty little blonde," Pulaski said. "Almost as purty as Miss Armand, but she don't speak much English. I understand she's Miss Armand's personal maid, but she's a part of the show, too. She comes out on stage and rings a bunch of bells. Not the sort of thing for a noisy saloon, but maybe the fellers'll sit still for it just to see Laurette."

"Well, you'd better get back to tackin' them posters up," Bolt said as he stepped aside. "Just leave the little fellow alone. You break his hands and Monte ain't gonna be too pleased with you."

"Yeah," Pulaski grumbled. He walked over and scooped his hat off the ground, dusted it off. "If you fellers are comin' to see Miss Armand sing tonight, you'd better come early. There won't be a seat left in the place by eight o'clock."

"I don't think we'll be there," Bolt said. "I hate crowds." He tugged on Tom's arm and the two friends walked on down the street, leaving the big man to pick up the flyers.

"Why don't we go see the show tonight?" Tom asked after they were away from Pulaski.

"Like I said, Tom, I don't like crowds. Especially noisy, shouting, shoving crowds of drooling drunks. And I don't like Monte Calhoun."

"Aw, come on, Bolt," Tom pleaded. "We owe it to ourselves to check it out. You heard what Pulaski said."

"I doubt that Clyde Pulaski is much of a judge of pretty women. Hell, look at him, Tom. Anything in skirts would look good to him."

"Then let's go find out for ourselves," Tom begged. "I'll even pay the dollar for you to get in."

"That's mighty sporting of you, Tom." Bolt thought about the drawing of the curvaceous singer.

He looked over at his friend and smiled. "All right, Tom, we'll go see if Laurette Armand is as pretty as her picture."

"Your curiosity got the best of you, didn't it?" Tom teased.

"Yeah, Tom," Bolt grinned, "I reckon it did."

CHAPTER TWO

Bolt and Tom arrived at the Prairie Schooner shortly before eight o'clock that night and were greeted by none other than Monte Calhoun himself.

When Calhoun spotted them entering the batwing doors, he pushed through the crowd toward them, a big smile on his face. Bolt knew the smile was phony, but he'd expected as much from a man with whom he shared a mutual dislike. It was the smugness of Monte's smile that bothered Bolt and made him sorry he'd allowed himself to be talked into attending this opening night fiasco.

Bolt choked on the thick cloud of cigar and cigarette smoke that hovered near the entrance and, when he saw the boisterous crowd that swelled the room to overflowing, he wanted to turn around and leave before Calhoun could reach them.

"Good evening, gentlemen," Calhoun said with a wide, toothy smile as he elbowed his way through the last knot of men who blocked his way to the entrance. "Bolt, Penrod," he said with an exaggerated nod to each man. He offered his hand, but Bolt turned away as if he hadn't seen it. Monte slapped his hands together. "Well, I must say I'm surprised to see you two here, but I'm glad you decided to come to see our beautiful Laurette Armand. You won't be disappointed. Look at this crowd, would you?"

Monte Calhoun was a tall, swaggering man with reddish brown hair, slicked back and parted in the middle. He was clean shaven and Bolt doubted that Monte was man enough to grow a moustache or a beard, or even hair on his chest, for that matter. He wasn't heavy by any means, but he seemed to have no waistline to speak of. He was just straight up and down and his trousers were always baggy in the rear where Calhoun didn't have enough buttocks to fill them out.

Monte usually wore dark trousers, a white shirt and a black string tie. He always wore an oversized cowboy hat and leather boots that were polished to a high shine. In colder weather, the saloon owner added a leather vest to his outfit, and sometimes a tailored buckskin jacket, complete with long, dangling fringe across the front and back, and along both sleeves. Calhoun was no more a cowboy than the Pope and although he looked like he had no muscles at all, Bolt knew better. He had tangled with Monte on two separate occasions and knew the saloon owner had a lot of power in his flabby looking body.

Tonight, Monte Calhoun wore a gaudy, gray plaid suit along with his regular leather cowboy boots and brown Stetson hat. Since he had no shape to begin with, he never looked sharp in the clothes he wore and the suit seemed too big for him because of his sloping shoulders. His string tie was red instead of the usual black. And, even without looking, Bolt knew that the trousers of the ostentatious suit were baggy in the rear.

"Hello, Monte," Bolt said. He quickly ignored the smug owner of the Prairie Schooner and made his way into the thick of the crowd, leaving Tom to pay the two dollars for their admission. Tom and Calhoun followed in his wake and came up behind him as Bolt stretched his neck and looked around for an empty table, or at least a couple of chairs where he and Tom could sit and watch the show.

At first glance, Bolt didn't see anything but a sea of loud, shoving, shouting rowdies who were primed for a good time. The saloon was dimly lit by glowing lanterns that hung from the rafters. Bolt hoped nobody would get drunk enough to start a fight. It would be hell to get out of there if the place caught on fire.

The long bar on the opposite side of the room was jammed with customers who pushed and yelled and elbowed each other in their struggle to get close enough to the counter to order a drink from the two overworked barkeeps.

As he scanned the room for a place to sit, Bolt saw that Calhoun had hired three waiters to take some of the load off the barkeeps. Dressed in white shirts and black trousers, the waiters held their heavy trays high above their heads as they tried to circulate through the crush of the crowd without being bumped. Each tray held a bottle of whiskey, a pitcher of foamy beer, and at least a dozen empty glasses.

Bolt didn't see anyplace where he and Tom could stand and watch the show without being jostled about in the crush of raucous men, unless they could stand along the wall. With the din of the noisy saloon ringing in his ears, Bolt had a sudden thirst for a good stiff shot of whiskey. But not one of the waiters was close enough for him to get a drink.

He glanced toward the bar again and decided it wasn't worth the effort. However, he did spot Clyde Pulaski among those rowdy men who swarmed around the bar. Poor bastard, he thought. Pulaski probably wouldn't be able to collect more than one of the free drinks promised to him by Monte Calhoun as payment for tacking up the flyers all over town. And like most of the others in the room, Pulaski wouldn't have a good seat to watch Laurette Armand's performance. Calhoun had used the big, burly man, plain and simple. As far as Bolt was concerned, it was just another indication of Calhoun's deceptive nature.

The stench of stale smoke and whiskey, spilled beer and musty sweat was overwhelming and Bolt tried not to breathe the smells into his nostrils. After he and Tom had eaten supper in a small cafe earlier that evening, they had stopped at the barbershop to get the stubble of whiskers shaved off their chins. The scent of their shaving lotion and hair tonic was now lost to the foulness of the air in the crowded saloon.

The loud clamor of raucous laughter and lewd

remarks, the din of clinking glasses and back-slapping and pushing and shoving was almost more than he could stomach and again, Bolt wished he'd stayed away.

Although Tom had grumbled about it, Bolt had made it clear beforehand that they wouldn't arrive at the Prairie Schooner until just before show time, and they would leave as soon as they had seen Miss Armand perform. Now he wondered if it was worth it at all and his tendency was to get away from the crushing crowd as fast as he could.

Monte Calhoun elbowed his way up to stand beside Bolt. "It's a shame you gentlemen didn't come earlier so you could have gotten a good seat," he said in a condescending manner as he made a big deal of glancing around the room in a phony effort to find them a place to sit. "As you can see, Laurette Armand has drawn a big crowd to the Prairie Schooner. I'm afraid you two will have to stand up to watch her performance, just like these other gentlemen."

Bolt didn't like the smug look of satisfaction on Calhoun's face and quelled the urge to punch the arrogant braggart in the nose. He knew that the pretentious saloon owner derived a great deal of pleasure in informing Bolt and Tom that, in order to see Miss Armand sing, they would have to stand among the loud, jostling, shoulder-to-shoulder crowd.

"That's all right," Tom said. "We ain't gonna be here that long. We'll just stand up against the wall over there."

"Fine, fine," said Calhoun with his toothy smile.

"You're both so intelligent, so cultured, I just know you're going to enjoy Miss Armand's performance."

"I'm sure we will. That is, if she's anything like you depicted her on your flyers," Bolt said sarcastically.

"I assure you, Bolt, Laurette is even more beautiful than that simple little pen-and-ink sketch you saw on the posters. And there was absolutely no way that I could portray her lovely voice on those flyers. You're in for a big surprise."

"I'll bet we are."

"Now, if you two gentlemen will excuse me," Calhoun said with a polite nod, "it's almost time for the show to begin and I must make my way up to the stage so I can introduce the entertainers."

"Oh, so that's why you're all gussied up tonight," Bolt said dryly.

"I'm surprised you noticed, Bolt. I hope your eyesight is also that good from a distance," Calhoun said, a biting edge to his words. "Otherwise you'll never be able to see how beautiful Miss Armand really is from way back here."

Again, Bolt had a powerful urge to knock that silly, sneering look off Calhoun's face. Instead he watched with delight as Calhoun turned away and bumped directly into the elbow of a fellow who was just about to take a drink. The glass of whiskey flew out of the customer's hand and the contents splashed in Calhoun's face and splattered across his new suit.

Calhoun whirled back around, blinking and wiping the strong drink from his eyes. The sharp aroma of whiskey rose all around Calhoun as he tried to brush the stain from his suit jacket.

Bolt ignored Calhoun's plight and turned away to

hide his smile. He stretched his neck and looked up at the low stage to judge how well he would be able to see Miss Armand from there. Not very well, he thought.

The stage was bare except for an upright piano on one side and a cloth-covered table on the other. Neatly arranged on the long white tablecloth were about two dozen hand bells in various sizes, brass bells with slender wooden handles. He saw that Monte Calhoun had hung a new, blue velvet curtain across the wall at the back of the stage. And where there had been only one short set of steps leading up to the stage, on the right side, Monte had added a second set of steps right in the middle. Other than that, Bolt saw no improvements in the old saloon.

If this Laurette Armand was supposed to be so special, a bouquet of fresh flowers on the stage would have been a nice touch, Bolt thought, or maybe a candelabra on the piano. Something to give the place a touch of class.

And then Bolt noticed the empty table and four vacant chairs near the stage. Front and center. The best seats in the house, he thought.

"There's an empty table up there," he said to Calhoun, who was still dabbing at his stained suit with a clean handkerchief.

"Where?" Calhoun called above the din of the noisy saloon as he looked up at Bolt.

"Up front," Bolt said in a loud voice. He stuck his arm up in the air and pointed toward the stage. "That'll do us just fine. Come on, Tom." He smiled and nodded to Monte, then started in that direction.

Calhoun grabbed his shoulder and stopped him.

"Oh, no. You can't sit up there, Bolt," he said with a look of horror and disgust that Bolt would even suggest such a thing. "You and Penrod will just have to stand back here with the other fellows who didn't bother to come here early enough to get a seat."

Bolt swung around and gave Monte a dirty look, then glanced down at his own shoulder where Calhoun's hand clutched his shirt. "Hands off," he warned.

Calhoun quickly dropped his arm. "I'm sorry, Bolt, but you can't sit up front," he said, regaining his composure. "That table is reserved."

"Oh, is that where you're going to sit?" Bolt asked sarcastically.

"No, I'll be far too busy with the show to sit down," Calhoun said, matching Bolt's sarcasm. "I'm saving that table in case someone really important comes in at the last minute."

"We'll take it, then," Bolt announced.

"Oh, no you won't," Calhoun said gruffly as he clenched his fist. "I said that table is reserved for someone important."

"Oh, I understand that, Monte. There's no problem at all." Bolt grinned and held up his hands as if to surrender to the saloon owner's wishes. He waited until Calhoun gave him another smug smile. "If the President or some other big shot comes in, we'll be more than happy to give up our front row table. C'mon, Tom." He spun on his heels and started toward the front of the saloon.

"You can't do that, Bolt," Calhoun protested. "Some of these fellows have offered me twenty dollars apiece for a seat at that ringside table. They'll be madder'n hell if I let you sit there."

"You should have taken the money while you had the chance," Bolt called over his shoulder at Calhoun, who stood in stunned silence, his mouth gaping open.

As he and Tom threaded their way through the noisy crowd, Bolt could feel the excitement building in the room as those who were standing jostled each other for the best view of the stage.

"How's this for good seats?" Bolt grinned as he and Tom sat down at the table closest to the center of the stage. He removed his Stetson and put it on the table, then glanced around at the other tables. He recognized a few of the neatly dressed men at the crowded tables as San Antonio businessmen, and he was willing to bet that each man had paid dearly for his place at the table. Monte would make a fortune tonight.

A waiter of Mexican descent came to their table almost immediately. He set the heavy tray down on the edge of the table. "Beer or whiskey?" he asked.

"We'll take whiskey," Bolt said as he dug into his pocket for money.

The waiter set two glasses in front of them, poured a healthy shot of whiskey in each glass. "One dollar," he said.

"A dollar for two drinks?" Bolt asked. "It used to be twenty-five cents for a drink. When did Monte raise his prices?"

"Tonight," the waiter said apologetically.

Bolt peeled off five dollars and placed them on the waiter's tray. "A dollar is for the drinks. The rest is for you, *amigo.*"

"Gracias," the Mexican said with a big smile as he stared wide-eyed at the money. "Here, you keep the bottle." He set the nearly full bottle of whiskey in the middle of the small table, picked up his tray and rushed off.

"See? He thinks we're important," Bolt laughed. "He's smarter than Monte is."

"Why'd you give him so much?" Tom asked.

"Because I figured he'd leave the bottle," Bolt laughed. "The money goes in his pocket, not Calhoun's."

"You got a lot of guts, Bolt." Tom looked over at his longtime friend and smiled.

"What do you mean?"

"Takin' this table when Calhoun said it was reserved."

"Hell, I didn't see any sense in letting this table go to waste. Besides, what can Monte do about it except maybe toss us out on our ass? No big loss if he did."

"You sure know how to get under his skin, Bolt," Tom said as he watched the stage anxiously.

"With a self-serving asshole like that, it's not hard to do."

"Jeez, for a minute there, I thought he was going to take a swing at you."

"Naw. Monte isn't going to start a fight and ruin his opening night," Bolt said.

"And speaking of Monte, here we go," Tom said, his voice full of enthusiastic anticipation.

Bolt glanced up and saw Calhoun making his way to the stage. A wave of excitement surged through the audience as the customers realized that the show was finally about to begin.

Bolt took a sip of whiskey and watched Monte Calhoun walk up the five steps on the right-hand side of the stage. "Baggy pants," he muttered to himself.

"What'd you say, Bolt?" Tom asked.

"Nothing, Tom."

Calhoun strutted across the stage in his gaudy new suit, his boots clanking against the wooden planks. He carried his cowboy hat in his hand and the five lanterns that lit the stage area made his slicked-back hair look even redder than it really was. The bright lamplight also accentuated the dark whiskey stain on the front of his gray suit jacket.

The loud, droning din of the raucous, impatient crowd settled down to a dull whir of whispers and clinking glasses.

"Good evening, gentlemen," Calhoun said in a loud booming voice. "Welcome to the newly remodeled Prairie Schooner. We have a very special treat for you tonight. The lovely, talented, sensual Miss Laurette Armand."

Calhoun paused dramatically, as if he expected the throng of lustful customers to respond. A few of the men applauded automatically. Others shouted lewd remarks or whistled their approval.

The pompous saloon owner glanced down at Bolt, a smug look on his face. When Bolt just sat there and stared at him, Calhoun looked out over the audience and raised his hand for silence before he continued.

"It gives me a great deal of pleasure to tell you that we were very fortunate indeed to be able to bring the famous Laurette Armand right here to the Prairie Schooner, direct from New Orleans. I know you're going to enjoy her."

A roaring cheer went up from the crowd.

Tom Penrod leaned over and whispered to Bolt, "Famous? Nobody ever heard of Laurette Armand before."

"No, but these fellows saw the flyers, same as we did," Bolt said in a loud whisper. "Calhoun had better produce this time or he's gonna have an angry mob on his hands."

Calhoun shot Bolt and Tom a dirty look.

"And you'll be first in line, Bolt," Tom said. "You and Monte are both spoiling for a fight."

"You're probably right, Tom." Bolt grinned.

CHAPTER THREE

Monte Calhoun swaggered across the stage and came back to the middle. The anxious customers began yelling for Laurette. Those who were standing in the back started shoving each other again, fighting for a better vantage point.

"Why doesn't he get on with it?" Tom asked as he leaned forward.

"Because he wants everyone to know how damned important he is," Bolt said.

"Gentlemen, quiet please," Calhoun shouted above the noise of the restless crowd. He held up both hands. "You'll get to meet Laurette soon enough. First, I'd like to introduce Miss Armand's pianist." He gestured toward the curtain behind the piano. "Mister Ken Selves."

The short, prissy piano player emerged from behind the end of the curtain and looked at his feet as he walked quickly to the center of the stage. He nodded once, then looked out at the audience, his eyes darting back and forth in their sockets. He had changed out of his gray, broadcloth suit and now wore a crisp black suit, a white shirt, and a black bow tie.

A smattering of polite applause rippled through the crowd.

Ken Selves looked like a penguin as he turned and took quick, short steps back to his piano, where he sat down and ran his fingers over the keyboard.

"I know you're all anxious to see Laurette Armand perform," Calhoun announced in his deep stage voice, "but first, we have a special treat for you. It gives me great pleasure to present another talented performer."

A few disgruntled boos arose from the restless throng of men in the back of the saloon.

"We want Laurette Armand," shouted one fellow who had obviously had too much to drink.

"Bring on Laurette," called another.

"We paid to see the pretty little sexy singer," yelled a burly fellow from the side of the room.

A few others joined in by stomping their feet and jeering.

"You're a phony, Calhoun," bellowed another.

Bolt felt the tension building in the room. He saw the flush of anger in Calhoun's cheeks and knew the saloon owner was struggling to keep his temper under control.

"If you fellows want to act like animals, why don't you go on outside with the mangy dogs?" Monte shouted. He waited until his customers gradually quieted down enough to listen to him. "Laurette Armand is in her dressing room right now, getting ready to entertain you. Miss Armand is a real lady and if you want her to come out here and sing for you, you're going to have to show me that you can act like gentlemen. Now, can we get on with the show?"

"Get on with it, then," shouted the troublesome burly man.

Calhoun waited until everyone was quiet. "Thank you. And now I'm pleased to present Miss Cherie Bonwit, who will entertain you with her concert of bells."

Several men shouted words of ridicule and displeasure that Laurette Armand was not going to perform right then.

Calhoun ignored the hecklers. "Miss Cherie Bonwit," he announced, gesturing toward the other end of the curtain.

When Cherie Bonwit stepped out on stage from behind the curtain, the shouts of ridicule quickly changed to cheers and ear-piercing whistles. Miss Bonwit was a pretty, petite blonde who looked the part of a French maid in her skimpy black outfit with its frilly white apron.

"Merci," Cherie Bonwit said timidly, her cheeks suddenly flushed with crimson. She curtsied and looked every bit as embarrassed and frightened as Ken Selves had when he came out on stage. As she walked toward her table of bells, she tugged self-consciously at her short skirt, as if she were trying to pull it down over her knees.

Bolt felt sorry for Miss Bonwit and figured that Monte Calhoun had forced her to wear the revealing costume. As he watched the swaggering saloon owner walk down the steps at the side of the stage, Bolt had nothing but contempt for Monte. It was obvious that Calhoun was exploiting the shy French girl and Bolt now wondered what Laurette Armand would be wearing when she performed on stage.

Poised behind the table, her legs hidden from view by the long, white tablecloth that hung clear to the floor, Cherie Bonwit picked up a bell in each hand, then glanced over at Ken Selves. The pianist played a fanfare and when he stopped, Cherie rang the two bells, set them down, quickly picked up two more and launched into a recognizable tune. Each bell had its own delicate tinkling sound.

"She's damned good," Bolt whispered, fascinated by the girl's talent.

"Yeah," said Tom, who stared at the girl in awe. "And she's damned pretty."

The idle chatter in the saloon gradually faded away as others became interested in Miss Bonwit's unusual musical performance.

With commanding concentration, Cherie picked up one bell after another, sometimes two at a time, skillfully creating a delightful, chiming tune.

The applause was spontaneous when she was through and she quickly launched into a more difficult tune. Her hands were a blur of movement as she reached for the various bells and, as far as Bolt could tell, she didn't miss a single note. He was impressed and it was evident by the cheering round of applause at the end of the tune that the others were, too.

Cherie Bonwit smiled shyly. *"Merci, merci,"* she said. And then she dashed to the curtain at the back of the stage and disappeared behind it.

"I've got to hand it to Monte," Bolt told Tom. "That was beautiful."

"Yes, she was," Tom sighed as he drank from his whiskey glass.

"I meant her playing, Tom."

"Yeah, that too." Tom grinned. "She can ring my bells anytime."

"You and every other randy fellow in here," Bolt replied. "Quit your droolin', Tom. It ain't fittin' for someone who's sittin' at this here table of honor to be actin' like a lecherous old fool."

"Hell, you can have Miss Armand. I'll take Cherie." Tom still pronounced it Cherry.

Monte Calhoun made his way back up on stage and strolled to the middle, his arms spread out to the audience. "Miss Cherie Bonwit. Wasn't she great?" he said, milking the audience for more applause. "And now for that special sexy lady you've all been waiting for, I'm proud to introduce the famous French *chanteuse,* Miss Laurette Armand." He gestured toward the middle of the blue velvet curtain.

The curtain jiggled and a hush of anticipation fell over the room as men strained their necks to see the stage.

Bolt leaned back in his chair and felt his heartbeat quicken as he was caught up in the excitement of the moment. He didn't watch Calhoun walk down from the stage this time, but continued to gaze at the curtain as it parted.

When Laurette Armand stepped through the curtains, Bolt's heart skipped a beat. Although he had seen the pen-and-ink drawing of her on the flyers, he wasn't prepared to see all of the fine details come to life. Her staggering beauty hit him right between the eyes. The young French singer was every bit as beautiful and curvaceous as the posters had depicted her. In fact, Laurette Armand was easily the most beautiful woman he'd ever seen.

Laurette was elegantly tall and slender, with hair as dark and shiny as a raven's wing, and eyes as blue as a clear mountain lake. She wore a tight, red silk gown that clung to her voluptuous figure as if it had been painted on and, as she walked, the long slit in the skirt parted to expose the flesh of her graceful legs. The long, slender sleeves of the gown were puffed at the shoulders, which drew Bolt's attention immediately to her pretty face. The front of the gown dipped down just far enough to show her ample cleavage.

The lines of her face were soft and delicate. She wore a hint of rouge on her high cheekbones and bright red lipstick on her full, sensual lips. Her dark raven hair was swept back away from her face and tied in back, held in place with a red ribbon. Soft, dark curls fell across her forehead, and the thin strands of hair that escaped from the bow hung in feathery wisps on both sides of her face.

An explosion of applause, interspersed with loud hollering and piercing whistles, rocked the room, nearly shattering Bolt's eardrums. He was glad he had this front-row seat. Not only was he away from the center of the raucous clamor that arose mostly from the men standing in the back of the room, but also, and more importantly, he had an unobstructed view of the stage, and of the lovely Laurette Armand.

Bolt's throat felt suddenly dry. He sat forward in his chair and took a sip of whiskey.

"She's beautiful, isn't she?" he whispered to Tom.

"Yeah," said Tom, his voice muffled by the noise of the excited crowd. He sat up tall in his chair. "Now, if she can sing, Monte's got himself a winner."

"Who cares if she can sing?" Bolt laughed nervously as he watched the singer walk toward the front of the stage, her long red skirt parting with every other step.

Unlike her two companions, who had seemed timid, Laurette Armand was totally poised on stage. She seemed to glide as she walked gracefully to the center of the stage, her red dress shimmering sensually in the lamplight.

"Thank you, gentlemen," she said with a dazzling smile that exposed sparkling white, even teeth. She curtsied graciously, then held both arms up in the air to acknowledge the applause, the long red sleeves of her gown as graceful as the way she held her hands. When she turned her head to nod and smile at the various sections of her audience, the long, dark curls at the back of her head skipped across her shoulders.

The crowd settled down immediately and when the room was quiet, Laurette repeated herself. "Thank you, *messieurs*. Gentlemen."

The sensual husk in her voice sent shivers across the back of Bolt's neck, as if someone had brushed a feather across his skin. A warm glow stirred through his loins and he felt like a young schoolboy falling in love for the very first time. He took a deep breath and tried to quell the funny feeling that roiled in his stomach.

"I am so happy to be here with you tonight, *messieurs*," Laurette said.

Again, the crowd hooted and applauded.

"Thank you," she said. And with just those two words, the men in the audience fell silent, as if she had waved a magic wand. "The first song I would like to sing was written for me by my pianist, *Monsieur* Selves. It is a ballad about a love left behind on the shores of France. I hope you will enjoy it. Ken." She nodded toward the short, introverted piano player who had sat idly at his piano during Cherie Bonwit's performance.

After Ken Selves played an introduction to the song, Laurette began to sing the plaintive ballad. She sang with the golden voice of a nightingale. From the very first note, her voice had a beautiful tone to it, a clarity that was rare, a husky sadness that touched Bolt's heart. She looked out at her audience as she sang and a couple of times, when she glanced down at Bolt, he felt himself melting inside.

When she finished the ballad, the applause and whistling and hollering was even more explosive than it had been when Laurette had first stepped out from behind the curtain. But, again, she had the power, by merely speaking, to quiet every voice in the room.

"*Merci, merci,*" she said with a bow of her head. "Thank you so much."

Laurette Armand sang another sad song and this time, it seemed to Bolt that she looked down at him more often. It was no wonder, he thought. He was so mesmerized by her that he couldn't take his eyes off of her. He was impressed with Ken Selves' playing, too, but he never looked over to watch the man play.

By the end of Laurette's second song, Bolt was beginning to feel a little uncomfortable under her gaze, especially when she flashed a smile at him. He felt flushed and hoped it didn't show. He applauded briefly with the others, then took a drink of whiskey. It didn't help to cool him down. It just added to his warm glow, and he wished he had a glass of water to wet his parched throat.

"And now I would like to sing one of my favorite songs in French," Laurette announced after three more tunes. "For you, *monsieur,*" she said with a big smile as she waltzed to the edge of the stage and extended her arm toward Bolt.

Other nearby customers strained to see who Miss Armand was talking to as the singer stepped back in place and waited for the musical introduction by Ken Selves.

Tom Penrod nudged Bolt with his elbow. "She likes you." He grinned.

"Shut up," Bolt whispered out of the corner of his mouth, wanting to crawl into a hole and disappear. He felt himself blush from his socks right on up to his cheeks and knew that if he hadn't been smitten with Laurette, the attention wouldn't have bothered him. Could she tell how he felt? No, he thought. Since Laurette was a beautiful woman, she had to be accustomed to men staring at her as Bolt had done. It had to be part of her act to single out the nearest customer to sing to.

Laurette broke into a lively French song and instead of singing it with a sad husk, there was a light, spirited lilt to her voice. She strolled back and forth across the stage as she sang, playing to her audience. When she sang the chorus of the song, she paused in front of Bolt and wiggled her hips as she looked down at him with a big, teasing smile.

Although they couldn't understand a word of the French song lyrics, the audience laughed and hooted at Laurette's suggestive movements. Bolt returned her smile, but felt like a fool. Each time Laurette came to that same phrase, she repeated her playful antics, and every time she dipped and wiggled her hips and smiled at Bolt, her actions drew a cheering response and more bawdy laughter from the customers of the saloon.

The audience loved her and, when the song ended, the room exploded with applause and loud hooting and whistling.

Laurette blew a kiss to Bolt, then raised her arms to her audience, graciously accepting their roaring applause.

"*Merci, merci.* Thank you, my friends," she said. "You are good people and I enjoy singing for you. And now, *Monsieur* Selves will play a short piano concert for you."

A few rowdy men booed and called out disparaging remarks.

"*Monsieur* Selves is a maestro," Laurette said. "If you will listen when he plays, you will like what you hear. And then, after he takes a short break, I will be back to sing for you again."

Miss Armand quickly retreated to her dressing room behind the curtains as Ken Selves began to play the piano. Although Selves was quite talented, the room buzzed with conversation and the noise of the customers moving about as they swarmed toward the bar to refill their drinks.

"Well, are you ready to leave?" Tom asked as he reached for his hat.

"Leave?" Bolt said. "What's your rush? We just got here."

"You said you didn't want to stay long."

"Well, I changed my mind."

"I thought so." Tom took his hand off his hat, settled back in the chair and grinned at his friend. "Quit drooling, Bolt. It ain't fittin'. . . ."

"I know," Bolt interrupted, "but I don't give a damn."

"Looks like Miss Armand has taken a fancy to you, Bolt," Tom said as he poured more whiskey for both of them. "You're the envy of every man here."

"Hogwash," Bolt said as he sat up straight and drank from the tumbler. "That's part of her act, Tom. She's a true professional and if she isn't famous, she sure as hell ought to be."

"She probably is famous in New Orleans."

"Ken Selves is pretty good, too. Better than any piano player I've ever heard." Bolt turned his attention to the short, prissy-looking pianist who was so wrapped up in his music, he didn't seem to care whether anyone was listening to him or not.

The music rolled off of Ken's fingers and filled that part of the room. Bolt became absorbed in watching the short man's fingers fly across the keyboard in some difficult movements. When Selves was through, he stood up, bowed quickly and disappeared behind the curtain. The small amount of applause he got came from the men who were seated at the tables.

"You're smitten with her, ain't you?" Tom asked after Ken was gone. He gave Bolt a knowing smile.

"Who? Laurette Armand? I don't even know her," Bolt said defensively. And then he grinned. "I'll admit, though, I wouldn't mind spendin' a little time gettin' to know her."

"You and every other randy fellow in the room," Tom said, giving Bolt back his own words.

"Including you, Tom."

"No, I prefer blondes. Cherry Bonwit is more my type." Tom chuckled.

"That figures."

"Monte Calhoun must think he's died and gone to heaven." Tom glanced up at the empty stage.

Bolt looked around the crowded room. "Yeah, Monte's finally got himself a class act. He'll draw the customers in here like flies to honey."

"That ain't what I meant, Bolt."

Bolt looked over at Tom, a puzzled expression on his face.

"I meant, I'll bet Calhoun is bedding both of them gals," Tom said. "I'll bet he's climbing the bones of both Laurette and Cherry."

"He'd better not be, the dirty bastard," Bolt said. "If he even thinks about it, I'll pound his face to pulp."

CHAPTER FOUR

A mob of unruly, loud-tongued customers crowded along the length of the long bar during intermission, pushing and shoving their way through the cluster of men who had stayed at the bar during the first half of Miss Armand's performance. The rowdy, merry men demanded drinks from the overworked barkeeps and made crude remarks to each other about what they would do if they could spend some time alone with the beautiful French singer.

Monte Calhoun stood with his friend, Ox Jarboe, at the end of the bar, the end closest to the stage, away from the crush of the jostling customers. From there, Monte could see the stage just fine by looking over the heads of those customers who were fortunate enough to be seated at one of the tables in the front of the room, including Bolt and Tom Penrod.

Calhoun and Ox Jarboe were like brothers in many ways, especially in the way they thought and acted, but as far as appearances went, they were complete opposites. While Calhoun was clean-shaven and made an attempt to look refined, Ox Jarboe, with his long, shaggy hair, his thick eyebrows and full beard and moustache, looked like he'd just come down out of the far shining mountains.

Jarboe, an uncouth ruffian, was a big hulk of a man with muscles that bulged his shirt. His dark feral eyes always seemed to have a mean, calculating look about them. Like Calhoun, Ox Jarboe spent more time dreaming up schemes to make easy money than he did actually working. And like Calhoun, he spent the money as fast as he got it and never seemed to have enough to make him happy.

The two big men had become friends several years before while they were both working as young cattle drovers for the same boss, and had discovered the similarities in their backgrounds. Both had come from wealthy, socially prominent families. Calhoun's father had been a cattle baron near Fort Worth and Jarboe's father owned a large cattle ranch near Abilene. Both Calhoun and Jarboe had rebelled against their domineering, tyrannical fathers and had run away from home as young lads to find their own fortunes in the west.

"Why in the hell was Laurette singing to Bolt, that sneaky little bastard?" Monte Calhoun complained during the brief intermission. He downed the whiskey in his glass and nodded to the closest barkeep, Sam Norris, for a refill.

"You ain't jealous, are ya, Monte?" Ox Jarboe laughed as he jabbed Calhoun with his elbow. He tipped his tumbler up and drank half a glass of beer in one swallow, then wiped the foam from his moustache with the back of his hand.

Sam poured more whiskey in Calhoun's tumbler, then took Jarboe's glass to refill it with beer.

"Why would I be jealous of that sonofabitch?" Monte snarled. "If Laurette knew that Bolt was an oily pimp, she wouldn't even look at him."

"Bolt ain't really a pimp," Ox said. "He and Tom just own a whorehouse."

"Same difference to me," Calhoun grumbled.

"Ah, hell, Monte," Ox said with a smile. "If you'd been able to turn the Prairie Schooner into a whorehouse like you wanted to, I wouldn't think of you as no oily pimp." He patted his friend on the shoulder.

Calhoun scowled into his glass, then took a healthy slug of the whiskey.

Sam Norris set the beer in front of Jarboe, then wiped the counter with a damp bar towel. "You know, Monte, you can't really blame Miss Armand for playing up to Bolt like that," he told his boss. Norris was a short, pudgy man, almost bald on top, with a thin moustache above equally thin lips. He was congenial and loyal and knew how far he could go with his boss when it came to offering free advice. Calhoun usually listened to him.

Monte gave the barkeep a dirty look. "Why, Sam? You think Bolt's handsome?" he said sarcastically.

"Bolt ain't all that bad-lookin'," Norris said. "Hell, if I were a woman, I'd probably think him handsome enough, in a rugged sort of way. But, that ain't what I meant, Monte, and you know it ain't."

"Then, what did you mean, Sam?" Calhoun picked up the stub of his cigar that had lost its fire and relit it, puffing several times until the cigar tip glowed bright red.

"Hell, Monte, you told Miss Armand that there'd be someone pretty important sitting at that front table. She probably figures she's doing you a favor by payin' special attention to him."

"She ain't doin' me no favors." Calhoun pouted. He took a drag on the expensive cigar, then blew a puff of smoke in the air. "If Laurette's got it in her pretty little head that Bolt is important, then I'd say that bitch is feathering her own nest, at my expense."

"That's no way to talk about a lady," Ox Jarboe laughed, a little tipsy from all the beer he'd consumed. "I thought you was sweet on Laurette."

"She's a business property. That's all," Monte said emphatically, even though it wasn't true. The fact was he had fallen hard for the beautiful Laurette and so far, she hadn't returned the favor. She was friendly enough to him, but she'd turned down all of his romantic advances. And now, he couldn't stand the thought of her making eyes at Bolt. Yes, he was jealous. Damned jealous.

"And a lucrative business property she is," Jarboe commented as he glanced around. "Just look at the crowd. She'll make you a fortune, Monte, and then you can sit back and enjoy life."

"Yeah, well, I just don't like Bolt and his sidekick nosin' around here," Calhoun said. "Them two jaspers are up to no good."

"Why in the hell did you let Bolt sit up there?" Sam Norris asked as he continued to polish the counter top.

"I didn't let him," Calhoun said. "That bastard bulled his way up there after I told him he couldn't sit there."

"Hell, I'd have tossed him out by the scruff of his balls if you'da just said somethin'." Jarboe laughed.

"I could have stopped both of those pushy jaspers by myself," Calhoun said as he stood up tall, "but I didn't want to cause any trouble tonight."

"Then I reckon you just got to live with that," Jarboe said.

"Yeah, well, Bolt had better keep his dirty paws off of her unless he wants to find out what trouble is," Calhoun snarled.

"Don't you be frettin' about him, Monte," Sam Norris said as he watched his boss drink down the whiskey. "If you just ignore Bolt and Penrod, there ain't gonna be no trouble tonight."

"Say, Monte, I've got an idea," Jarboe said. He leaned against the bar and swirled the beer around in his glass. "If you still want me to be a partner in the Prairie Schooner, I know how we can turn this place into the fanciest saloon in the west."

"How's that?" Calhoun asked sullenly.

"We'll expand." Ox Jarboe set his glass down, turned and looked around the room. "We'll double the size to begin with and add enough tables and chairs so everyone can sit down. Then, we'll buy up the rest of the block and build a fancy hotel where the pretty little chambermaids will actually be high-class prostitutes."

"That'll take money, Ox, and right now, I don't have much of it."

"I've got a little cash to get us started on the expansion," Jarboe said, "but that's where my brilliant plan comes into play."

"What kind of a scheme have you cooked up this time?" Calhoun asked with a tone of skepticism in his voice. He stubbed out his cigar in a clay ashtray.

"It'll work, Monte," Jarboe said with a devilish grin. "We'll hold a raffle every night. We'll sell tickets all evening and I'll bet you we'll take in as much money from the raffles as we do from that rotgut booze you sell."

"And just what are we going to raffle?" Calhoun snorted. He drank down the rest of the whiskey and set his glass on the counter, waving Sam Norris off when the barkeep offered to refill it.

"That's the best part of it," Jarboe said with glee as he rubbed his hands together. "We'll raffle off something different every night. A bottle of booze one night, maybe a new Stetson hat the next night, or silver spurs, or a cow. Hell, the possibilities are endless."

Calhoun rubbed his chin. "Might work."

"Wait, you haven't heard the best part." Jarboe looked around to make sure no one was listening, then spoke in a low voice. "After we get the hotel built, then every Saturday night we'll raffle off a free night's lodging that will include the services of a pretty little chambermaid. You don't think we'll sell raffle tickets with that? We'll be rich, Monte," he said as he slapped his friend on the back.

"Well, I'll be damned, Ox, I think you came up with a winner this time," Calhoun said with a big grin. "Yeah, we're gonna be rich."

Sam Norris reached over the counter and tapped Monte on the arm. "Pardon me, boss, but the natives are getting restless. If you don't get Miss Armand back up there on stage right away, the customers are gonna start walkin' out of here and your dreams of wealth will go up in smoke."

Calhoun glanced around and saw that the crowd had become impatient. "Yeah, I'd better get up there and bring her back out." He grabbed his hat, positioned it on his head and made his way toward the front.

When Laurette Armand came back on stage a few minutes later, almost every man in the room turned his attention to the beautiful singer.

Monte Calhoun didn't bother to take off his hat this time. He gave Bolt a dirty look, then lifted his head proudly. "Thank you, gentlemen," he said in a booming voice. "I'm glad you all like Miss Armand." After a roar of applause, he glanced at Bolt smugly, then continued. "I'm already making plans to expand this place, and with Laurette Armand here, the Prairie Schooner will soon become the most famous saloon in all the West."

Bolt felt his temper flare when Calhoun reached down and took Laurette's small, graceful hand in his own oversized paw and smiled at her. He wondered if that bastard was taking Miss Armand to his bed. No, he thought, Laurette had more class than to sleep with a scumbag like Monte Calhoun.

"And, now, the famous Laurette Armand will sing for you again," Calhoun announced. He squeezed Laurette's hand, held it in the air as he looked down at Bolt, an arrogant smile on his face.

Bolt knew that Monte was making it perfectly clear to him that he owned the singer. Well, Monte didn't own shit, Bolt thought.

Laurette slipped her hand away from Calhoun's grasp, folded her hands in front of her and bowed to the audience. Calhoun turned and made his way off the stage.

Bolt leaned over to Tom as Ken Selves began playing the introduction to Laurette's next song. "What would you say if I hired Miss Armand to sing at our place?" he whispered.

Tom turned to Bolt, a scowl on his face. "Laurette singing at a bordello?" Tom whispered. "I'd say you were asking for a heap of trouble from Calhoun."

"Just a thought." Bolt grinned. "I'd sure as hell like to get her away from here."

"Don't even think it," Tom said as he shook his head. He turned his attention back to the stage.

"It don't hurt to dream," Bolt sighed as Miss Armand began to sing.

"In your case, it's downright dangerous," Tom grumbled with a sideways glance.

Bolt ignored his friend's remarks as Laurette Armand's golden voice swelled around him like the sound of a harmonious orchestra. Her voice was a delicate musical instrument. It was all musical instruments blended together.

Totally fascinated by the beautiful, blue-eyed French singer, he watched Laurette's every movement and noticed how her snug red gown shimmered when her hips swayed. The cleavage of her clinging dress showed only a hint of her smooth breasts, but it was enough to tantalize Bolt. As she strolled along the front of the stage, singing to her audience, the split in her skirt kept flashing open, exposing the sensual bare flesh of her long, graceful legs.

Damn, it was almost more than a man could bear to watch her, Bolt thought, and he knew he wasn't the only one in the room who felt that way about Laurette. Although some of the customers at the back of the room were feeling the effects from heavy drink and were noisier than before, they were still much quieter than they normally would have been. The distraction of the added noise in the room didn't seem to bother Miss Armand and she carried on like a trouper.

Laurette sang a medley of popular tunes, varying them between the soft, plaintive ballads of lost loves, the down-south folk songs, and the more lively tunes that always brought a thundering response from the audience.

While she was singing, Laurette looked down at Bolt often enough to make him feel self-conscious and uncomfortable. Although there were times when he wanted to slink down in his chair and look away from her, he was drawn to her haunting beauty like a magnet and never did take his eyes off her.

Bolt didn't know where Monte Calhoun was standing, or sitting, nor did he care, but he could almost feel the saloon owner constantly glaring at him. Wherever Calhoun was, he had to notice that Laurette was paying special attention to Bolt because it was so obvious that she was singing directly to him a good part of the time. Or was it that obvious to anyone else? Maybe all the customers felt the same way Bolt did. Maybe Laurette had the ability to make every man in the room feel like she was singing directly to him.

Bolt applauded with the others, but he was so rattled by Laurette's beauty that he could barely think straight enough to know that she had just finished singing another song. He felt somewhat relieved when she looked out over the audience.

"Thank you, gentlemen," Laurette said with a big smile. "And now, for my last number this evening, I would like to sing for you one of my favorites, "A Bird in a Gilded Cage." I hope you enjoy it."

Laurette's voice was as clear as a crystal bell and so sweet and beautiful that Bolt felt a chill run down his spine. Ken Selves played the piano masterfully and kept the music low enough under Laurette's voice so that he didn't overshadow her.

Bolt melted inside when Laurette glanced down at him and smiled. Although she sang the song in a breezy, lighthearted manner, he could hear the sadness in her voice. He could see it in her deep blue eyes. He sensed that she felt trapped in her own gilded cage and it was almost as if she were pleading with him to help her get free. Was he imagining these things? Probably so. He had a sudden urge to become her savior, but he recognized that it was just a feeling stirring inside him that she invoked with her husky voice.

There was a deadly silence in the room when she ended her song on a deep, low note and then the room exploded with hearty applause and shrill whistles of approval.

"Merci," Laurette called out above the noise. She extended her arms to the skies. "Thank you so much.

Thank you," she said, bowing to each section.

"More! More!" shouted some of the men.

"Thank you, gentlemen," she said. "You have been a wonderful audience. I hope you will come back."

The cheering and clapping went on as Monte Calhoun made his way to the steps at the far end of the stage.

On a sudden impulse, Bolt scooted his chair back, stood up and headed for the stage.

"Where in the hell are you going?" Tom said. He grabbed his hat off the table and stood up, prepared to leave.

Bolt didn't glance back at Tom. He rushed over and stood below the stage, next to the steps in the middle, and looked up at Laurette.

"Pardon me, Miss Armand. Would you care to join me at my table?" he asked, hoping she wouldn't consider him too bold. "I'd be honored if you'd sit and talk to me and my friend for a spell."

Laurette looked at him for a minute, then broke out in a smile. *"Oui, monsieur.* Yes. It would be my pleasure."

As Laurette started down the center steps, Bolt quickly offered her his hand. He glanced over and saw that Monte Calhoun had just then stepped up onto the stage from the far steps. Monte glared at him, a stunned look of disbelief in his eyes.

Bolt hadn't expected Laurette's hand to be so soft and warm and the sensation of actually touching her made his knees go weak as he helped her down the steps. The scent of her heady perfume wrapped around him like an aromatic cloud of freshly crushed dried flowers.

"My name's Bolt," he said. He drank in her sweet smell as he escorted her to his nearby table.

"Just Bolt?" she asked with a coy smile.

"It's Jared Bolt, but everyone calls me Bolt. And this is my friend, Tom Penrod," he said as he pulled out a chair for her. In her tight red gown, Laurette seemed to slither gracefully into the chair Bolt offered her and, after she was seated, Bolt and Tom sat down on either side of her.

"*Monsieur* Bolt, *Monsieur* Penrod. It is my pleasure to meet you," she said with a demure smile that tugged at Bolt's heart.

Monte Calhoun was at center stage by now, just above Bolt's table. His eyes flashed with hatred as he looked down at the trio.

"Thank you, Miss Armand," he said loudly. He glowered at Bolt, but Bolt just turned his attention to the beautiful woman sitting beside him.

Calhoun thanked Ken Selves, who stood up and took a bow. Then Monte called Cherie Bonwit back on stage for a round of applause for her performance. After a brief curtsy, Miss Bonwit walked and stood beside Ken Selves. Calhoun droned on, bragging about the greatness of the Prairie Schooner and his plans for expansion, his dreams of making it the most famous saloon in all the West. When he saw that nobody was paying any attention to him, he finally gave up and left the stage, glaring at Bolt one last time.

"You have a lovely voice, Miss Armand," Bolt said, glad that Calhoun hadn't tried to drag Laurette away from his table.

"Thank you. I hope you will both come back tomorrow night," she said, her voice just as musical when she spoke as when she sang.

"We just might," Bolt said.

"Would your friend, Cherry Bonwit, like to join us?" Tom asked. He nodded toward the stage where Selves and Cherie were talking to each other.

"She pronounces it Chérie," Laurette giggled. "Perhaps another night, *Monsieur* Penrod. It is late and we are all still tired from our long journey. I hope you will both forgive me if I do not stay long."

"We understand," Bolt said. "Are you staying at the Alamo Hotel?"

"*Oui*. For now we are staying at the hotel, but soon we will be looking for a suitable house."

"What made you come to the wide open prairie of San Antonio from the beautiful seaport of New Orleans?" Bolt asked.

"New Orleans is beautiful, yes," Laurette said, "but, alas, it has become crowded and there are now many unsavory characters roaming the streets there. When Mr. Calhoun offered me a job here, I thought it would be nice to come to the open country where it is quiet and serene."

"It is peaceful out in the country where we live," Bolt said with a smile, "but we have ruffians here in San Antonio, too."

"Some of them right here in this very saloon," Tom added.

"I must admit, I had some qualms about working in a saloon when *Monsieur* Calhoun offered me this job," Miss Armand said. "I don't mean to sound uppity, but I've always performed in theaters before and I thought the type of men who frequent saloons might be too crude for my likings."

"These fellows are on their best behavior tonight." Bolt smiled and felt all funny inside when he looked into Laurette's sparkling blue eyes. "Not often do they get the chance to see a woman as beautiful as yourself." He resisted the urge to reach across the table and touch her delicate hand.

"Why, thank you, Mr. Bolt," she smiled coyly. "What do you two gentlemen do here in San Antonio?"

"We have a cattle ranch south of town," Bolt replied.

"Oh, I would just love to see a real cattle ranch sometime," she cooed.

"You're welcome at the Rocking Bar Ranch anytime," Bolt said. "We'll show you around."

"I would really like that," she said. "And now, if you'll excuse me, I really must go. It is late and Cherie is waiting for me."

"Would you like us to walk you to the hotel, Miss Armand?" Bolt suggested. "As you say, it's late, and it might not be safe for you two beautiful women to be out on the street alone this time of night."

"Thank you for your kind offer, *Monsieur* Bolt, but it won't be necessary," Laurette said. "My pianist, Ken Selves, is staying at the hotel, too, and he will escort us back there. Cherie and I will feel quite safe with Ken by our sides."

"Are you sure, ma'am?" Bolt asked. "Pardon me for saying so, but Mr. Selves doesn't look like he could offer you much protection."

Laurette smiled. "Oh, I know Ken doesn't look like he could be very strong, but he really is. Most people assume he's a coward because of the way he looks, but he's the bravest man I know."

"Ken Selves is brave?" Tom asked. He glanced at Bolt and rolled his eyes upward.

"Mercy, yes," Laurette said. "Ken would give up his life to protect us if he had to."

"Well, I'm sure it won't come to that." Bolt laughed. "The hotel is just a block away."

Laurette smiled at him and he felt giddy when he saw the teasing look in her big, blue eyes. He wondered if she was flirting with him.

"I know," she said. "I'm sure we'll be quite safe."

Bolt's mood changed instantly when he saw Monte Calhoun marching toward their table. Monte was wearing his oversized Stetson now and walking behind Calhoun was that big-boned fellow, Ox Jarboe, followed by one of Calhoun's barkeeps, Sam Norris.

"Get up, Miss Armand," Monte said gruffly when he reached the table. "You're through for the evening, so go on."

"What do you mean?" she asked, a puzzled look on her face.

"I mean I don't want you sitting here with these two jaspers."

Laurette looked at Bolt and Tom, then back at her boss. "Why, *Monsieur* Calhoun?" she asked innocently. "You told me that they were very important men in this town. I was just talking to them."

"Why, Mr. Calhoun," Bolt grinned, "that was nice

of you to speak so kindly about us."

"Don't get funny with me, Bolt, you pushy bastard," Calhoun snapped. His face turned brick red. "Laurette, this man is little better than a goddamned pimp."

Harsh words in a western town.

Fighting words, as far as Bolt was concerned.

CHAPTER FIVE

Laurette Armand stared up at Monte Calhoun, her innocent blue eyes suddenly wide with surprise. Her sensual red lips formed a small "O" and she quickly covered her mouth with her hands as she looked over at Bolt.

Bolt couldn't tell whether the beautiful singer was shocked by Calhoun's crude language or by the fact that Bolt might possibly be a pimp, if the saloon owner's words were true.

"That isn't true about me, Calhoun," he said as he pushed his chair back. He stood up, stepped away from the table, his eyes narrowed to slits.

Tom jumped up from the table when Jarboe and Sam Norris walked up and stood next to Calhoun. "Let it go, Bolt," he pleaded. "It ain't worth it."

"I won't let it go," Bolt said as he glared at the pompous saloon owner. "I don't care what you say about me, Calhoun, but you've got no right to talk that way to a lady."

"No different from the way you talk to your filthy

whores, Bolt," Calhoun laughed.

"Not true. You don't know how to act in front of a lady because you've never known a real lady before," Bolt accused.

"Look, this is my place, Bolt, and don't you forget it, you dumb bastard," Calhoun said bravely as he strolled up to Bolt. "Laurette works for me and I'll talk to her any damned way I want to."

"Not while I'm around," Bolt said. He stood with his arms hanging loosely by his sides. He felt a fight brewing, but he'd be damned if he'd be pushed into throwing the first punch. "You owe Miss Armand here an apology."

"You think you're big enough to make me, you dirty sonofabitch?" Calhoun doubled up his fist and shook it in Bolt's face.

"If I have to," Bolt said calmly as he remained firm in his stance. "I'm certainly not afraid of tangling it up with a pip-squeak like you."

"Oh, yeah? You talk big, Bolt, but you're a damned coward." Calhoun drew his fist back, threatening to punch Bolt in the face.

Laurette Armand rose from the table and rushed over to the edge of the stage. Ken Selves and Cherie Bonwit scrambled down the steps and stood beside her.

Chairs screeched across the floor as the men at nearby tables got up and cleared away from the immediate area, carrying their drinks with them. Other customers who were farther away turned their heads toward the commotion near the stage.

"Fight! Fight," called someone from the back of the room.

"Where?" hollered another.

"Up there," said someone else.

"So you want to fight?" Monte Calhoun yelled as he bounced up and down, his weight shifting from one foot to the other, both hands drawn into tight fists.

"No, Calhoun, I don't want to fight," Bolt said. "I want you to apologize to Miss Armand."

"I thought so, you slimy pimp," Calhoun shouted, ignoring Bolt's remarks. He took a fighter's crouch, one hand in front of the other. "I knew you was gonna be trouble the minute you walked in here."

"You apologize to Miss Armand, Calhoun, and Tom and I will leave quietly," Bolt said.

"The hell you will." Calhoun drew back a fist and threw a hard punch at Bolt's face.

A little cry of startled fear escaped Laurette's lips.

Bolt blocked the blow with his arm and plowed into Monte's jaw with an uppercut.

The saloon owner gasped as his head snapped back. His hat sailed off his head and he staggered backwards a few steps. Ox Jarboe and Sam Norris rushed in to steady Calhoun.

Tom Penrod watched carefully. He wouldn't interfere as long as it was an even fight, one-on-one, but if either Jarboe or the hefty barkeep got into it, he would jump into the fray.

Bolt waited, both fists cocked.

Calhoun came at him again, swinging with both hands. "You dirty bastard!" he shouted.

Bolt ducked the first blow, attacked with a hard punch of his own, then dodged the second driving fist. Both men missed, but kept thrashing at each other with powerful thrusts, each scoring damaging blows, knocking over chairs that got in their way, overturning a couple of tables in their path.

Those customers closest to the brawling men pushed back away even farther and were soon caught in the crush of the unruly customers who were crowding toward the front in order to see better. The grunts and groans of the two fighters were muffled by the sounds of scuffling feet and the screeching of the tables and chairs that were being pushed aside.

Calhoun was finally able to get the advantage and plowed into Bolt's chest with a hard right, knocking Bolt backwards into a straight-backed chair. One leg of the chair splintered off with a loud crack and the chair clattered to the floor, snapping another wooden leg in half.

Still flying backwards, Bolt tripped over the fallen chair and got his feet all tangled up in the rungs of the chair legs. His arms flailed the air as he teetered for a brief moment, sure he was going to go down. He pawed the air harder, got his feet free from the tangle of wooden rungs and finally managed to regain his balance.

Calhoun was on him like a pouncing panther.

Laurette Armand gasped and clutched Cherie Bonwit's arm as the two girls huddled together below the stage. Ken Selves watched the fight with rapt fascination.

Bolt saw Calhoun coming toward him again and ducked his head to the side just as the saloon owner's fist sailed right on by his ear. As Monte's clean-shaven face loomed up in front of his own, Bolt pulled his fist back and then drove it forward with all of his strength, plowing it into Calhoun's lurching face. He missed Calhoun's nose, but felt the flesh of Calhoun's cheek give under the force of his blow. An instant later, when Calhoun raised his head, Bolt saw the blood that trickled from a thin cut on Monte's cheekbone.

"You fuckin' bastard," Calhoun shouted, dabbing at the small gash with the back of his hand.

Aroused by the first sight of blood, the boisterous crowd encouraged the fight by cheering and booing, depending on which man they were rooting for. One enterprising fellow started to take bets from those who were willing to put up the money.

Bolt moved in fast. He punched Calhoun in the stomach and followed it up with a hard jab to the man's chin. The force of the blow sent Calhoun reeling backwards and he crashed into a nearby table. As the table scooted across the wooden planks with a nerve-shattering screeching noise, an empty tumbler slid off the table and smashed to the floor with a loud crash, followed by the tinkling of shattering glass.

Off balance, Calhoun held both hands in front of him as Bolt pressed his advantage and lunged toward the saloon owner.

Tom Penrod saw Ox Jarboe grab the whiskey bottle off the table where he and Bolt had been sitting and then go after Bolt from behind. Tom jumped in and jerked Jarboe's arm back just as the bearded ruffian was about to crack the bottle over Bolt's head. The nearly full glass container slipped from Jarboe's clutches and smashed to the ground, spraying whiskey and shards of glass all over the floor and onto the trousers of the fighters.

When Jarboe spun around, a startled look in his dark, beady eyes, Tom let him have it with a hard knee to the groin. Tom followed it up by shoving a hard fist into Jarboe's bearded chin.

Ox Jarboe grunted and collapsed to the floor, clutching his crotch as he rolled back and forth, groaning in agony. Tom Penrod stood over him, threatening to drive a boot into the big man's groin if he tried to get up.

Sam Norris, the pudgy barkeep, snatched up one of the broken chair legs off the floor. He snuck up behind Tom and slammed the clublike weapon into the back of Tom's head.

Laurette Armand shuddered. Cherie Bonwit squealed and covered her eyes.

The crowd shouted but Tom never heard them. For a brief instant, he saw bright, colorful stars dancing in his head. And then a dark cloud seemed to wrap round him and he felt like he was falling through a bottomless black tunnel as he crumpled to the floor, unconscious from the brutal blow.

Ox Jarboe picked himself up slowly and limped away from the melee, still holding his aching crotch. Sam Norris stood firm, the splintered chair leg in his upraised hand, threatening to use it on anyone else who decided to enter the fight that was between Bolt and Monte Calhoun.

Another scuffle erupted in the back of the room as drunken customers argued about who was fighting fair and who wasn't.

Unaware of what was going on behind his back,

Bolt continued to exchange punches with the unrelenting saloon owner, who had regained his balance and attacked Bolt with a renewed vengeance. In the thick of the fist fight, he was remembering all too painfully that Calhoun was a good, strong fighter.

Winded from his efforts, Bolt drove his fist into Calhoun's stomach and then struck again with a loud, thudding blow to Calhoun's jaw.

Calhoun countered with a powerful wallop to Bolt's cheek.

Bolt felt his face twist out of shape as Calhoun's fist pounded into soft flesh. He ignored the pain that seared through his brain and went after Calhoun with both fists flying. He connected with a crushing blow to the corner of Calhoun's eye, then slammed his other hammering fist into Monte's throat.

Calhoun coughed and sputtered, then lunged forward and grabbed Bolt around the neck with both of his powerful hands.

Bolt felt Monte's forceful grip tighten around his windpipe. He gasped for air, but couldn't suck any into his lungs. A shroud of darkness started to close in on him. With his last bit of consciousness, he brought both arms up hard and whacked Calhoun's grasping hands away from his throat. Air rushed to his lungs and, for a minute, he felt light-headed.

He jumped back away from the saloon owner and, out of the corner of his eye, he noticed the limp body stretched out on the floor a few feet away. He turned his head and glanced down, stunned to see that it was his friend, Tom Penrod, on the floor. Unconscious or dead—he didn't know which.

Bolt's heart fluttered when he saw the small puddle near Tom's head. At first glance, he thought it was blood. In the dim light on the floor, it was hard to tell. And then, just as he smelled the sharp, heavy stench of alcohol, he noticed the shards of broken glass on the floor and quickly realized that the puddle was whiskey, spilled from a broken bottle. He stared down long enough to see Tom's chest rise and fall with his slow, even breathing.

Bolt turned back just in time to see Calhoun's doubled-up fist plunging toward his face. He didn't have time to duck away from the attacking hamhock of a fist and he caught the stunning blow square across his jaw with a bone-crunching, neck-twisting force. His brain exploded with pain and, for a brief moment, he couldn't even think.

From somewhere deep inside, he sensed that Calhoun was about to strike again. He shook his head, trying to clear the cobwebs from his mind in time to fend off another blow. He winced with the pain that sliced through to the core of his brain, certain that his neck was broken. He grabbed his neck and groaned, staggered backwards, his eyelids drooping.

Groggy, Bolt instinctively dodged the mass hurtling toward him.

Calhoun, putting all his force behind his thrust, sailed on by Bolt and slammed into a table. He whirled around, started back toward Bolt and tripped over a chair that had been knocked over earlier. His hands clawed at the air, but he lost his balance and slammed to the floor, breaking his fall with the palms of his hands.

Blinded by pain, Bolt shook his head again, then went after the downed man just as Calhoun scrambled to his feet. He jammed a fist into Monte's face, struck him hard on the side of his chin.

Calhoun staggered backwards with the force of the blow and tripped over the same chair. This time he landed on the back of his head, which stunned him momentarily.

When Bolt saw that Monte wasn't moving, he rushed over to Tom Penrod and crouched over him. "Tom. Tom," he yelled as he shook his friend's shoulder. "Are you all right?" Tom didn't respond. Bolt slapped his cheeks. "Come on, Tom, wake up."

Tom's eyelids fluttered open and he stared up at Bolt. "What the . . ." He started to raise his head but was driven back to the floor by the excruciating pain at the back of his head.

Shouts of warning rose above the rumble of the cheers and jeers. Bolt whirled around just in time to see Calhoun coming at him, a chair raised over his head. He dropped to the floor and rolled out of the way just as Monte swung the chair down with full force. Bolt cringed at the loud snapping sound of two of the chair legs splintering off from their base, grateful that he had been able to dodge the crushing blow.

Calhoun, furious that he had missed, dropped the broken chair and went after Bolt, both fists swinging, his face red as a beet.

Bolt jumped up and was ready for the renewed attack against him. He warded off several blows and took a right to his chin before he was able to connect with an uppercut to Calhoun's jaw. Equally matched in strength and fighting ability, the two adversaries danced in a slow circle, parrying as they each struggled for the advantage that would put an end to the other. The fight soon became a game of wits and the only sounds in that part of the room were the scuffling of their boots scraping against the floor, their grunts and groans as blows were exchanged, and the occasional shouts of encouragement from the bloodthirsty onlookers.

Circling, Bolt finally saw his chance to get the upper hand. He tightened his stomach muscles and intentionally took a low blow to his gut. As Calhoun drew his fist back from Bolt's belly, Bolt drove a hard fist square into the saloon owner's nose.

Calhoun yelped and backed away from his attacker. He moaned and reached for his nose. Blood spurted from both nostrils, oozing through Monte's fingers. He staggered back and leaned against a table, his breath coming in short pants.

Equally winded from the exertion, Bolt stepped back and let his weight sag against another table. With sweat trickling down his forehead, he stood there for a minute, one hand on the table, one on his chest, as he gasped for air. Every muscle in his body ached as he eyed his opponent. He glanced over and saw that Tom had pulled himself up into a chair and was sitting there, his aching head in his hands.

Bolt expected Calhoun to pounce on him again right away, but the weary saloon owner stayed where he was, moaning and holding his injured nose. Bolt wondered if he'd broken Calhoun's nose, but he didn't really care at this point. He was just grateful for the brief respite to catch his breath.

After a short rest, both men were ready to tangle it up again. They put up their fists and started toward each other when Laurette Armand walked over and stood between them.

"Stop it," she said, both hands held up. She glanced sternly at each of them. "Stop it, you overgrown fools."

Both men backed off obediently.

"For shame," she scolded, "two grown men fighting. Over little me? Nonsense. I care nothing for either of you."

With that, Laurette spun around and strutted off, the heels of her high-button shoes clacking across the wooden planks of the floor.

Bolt and Monte Calhoun glared at each other for a long minute, as if determining whether to continue the fight or not. But for Bolt, the fight didn't seem important anymore. Without Laurette there, he had no reason to fight and beating up Calhoun wasn't worth the effort.

He turned away and walked over to his table, snatched up both his hat and Tom's.

"C'mon, Tom, let's get out of this rat hole," he said as he handed Tom his hat.

Tom got up slowly and the two friends started toward the door as the grumbling, disappointed crowd stepped aside to let them pass.

"I want you two trouble-makin' bastards out of here," Monte Calhoun called after them, still cupping his bleeding nose. "And don't you ever set foot in the Prairie Schooner again."

Bolt didn't reply to the ranting man. He didn't even turn around to give him a dirty look. He didn't want to give Calhoun the satisfaction of knowing that he heard him.

Outside, the cool night air washed across his hot, sweaty face like a cleansing rag. Away from the brawling, the smoke, the stench of whiskey and beer, and the confusion of the noisy crowd, his head began to clear.

He realized how much Laurette's words had stung him. She cared nothing for him, she had said, and those simple words had taken all the fire out of him.

He realized, too, how much he was smitten by the raven-haired beauty who sang with the golden voice of a nightingale.

CHAPTER SIX

"What in the hell are you doing now, Bolt?" Tom Penrod asked as he strolled from the kitchen hallway into the large, ornately decorated sitting room of the Rocking Bar Bordello.

The bordello was actually a big, old, two-story house on Bolt and Tom's ranch where the six harlots who worked for them lived. Harmony Sanchez, the pretty, young woman who served as madam, housemother and friend to the girls, lived there, too, in the downstairs living quarters at the back of the house. At night, the big front sitting room became the main gathering place for the customers who came to avail themselves of the services of the harlots.

There was a long, mahogany bar at one end of the room, a small stage near the bar, a piano on the floor below the platform. On the other side of the room were two plush, velvet sofas facing each other in the center of the area, with a low table between them, several comfortable chairs scattered around, and along the walls, some hard-back chairs. The small game table that sat in the corner of the room, beyond the sofas, was often used by customers who played poker or dominoes while they waited for their turn with a favorite soiled dove.

Each girl had her own bedroom upstairs, but the harlots did not bed their customers up there. The girls met the men in the big sitting room where they socialized with them, talked with them, teased them, and danced with them sometimes. But when it came time to pleasure the men, each girl took her customer to one of the charming, individual cottages out in back of the big house.

Bolt and Tom lived in the big, rambling ranch house near the entrance to the ranch property, up the hill from the bordello. Their two ranch hands, young Chet Ralston and a big burly fellow named Rusty, lived in the long bunkhouse near the stable.

Bolt credited Harmony Sanchez with the smooth running of both households and the bordello. Besides serving as the madam of the whorehouse at night and running a cheerful home for the girls when they weren't working, Harmony kept Bolt and Tom's house spotless. In addition to that, she did the laundry for Bolt and Tom, mended their clothes and cooked for them when they didn't share their meals with the girls.

Tom had been nursing the painful bump on his head for four days now, basking in the special attention given to him by all of the girls who worked at the bordello. It was the middle of the afternoon and he had just finished drinking a cup of hot sassafras tea that one of the harlots had fixed for him.

"Jeeez, that damned pounding of yours is hurting my poor old head." He pressed both of his hands against his head as if to emphasize his point.

Bolt paused, hammer in hand, as he leaned over the boards he was adding to the small stage.

"Good, I'm glad you're here, Tom," he said. "I can use your help."

"But, my head," Tom grumbled.

"You're playing it for all the sympathy you can get, aren't you?" Bolt laughed. "It's time to stop moping around and get back to work."

"You should talk," Tom said. "You're the one who's been moping around here for the past four days. Hell, why don't you go see her?"

"See who?" Bolt asked with a look of innocence.

"You know damned well who," Tom said. "Laurette Armand. Why don't you go see her and get it out of your system?"

"Because I'm not setting foot inside the Prairie Schooner again. Ever."

"Well, you'd better do something. Ever since Laurette Armand told you she wasn't interested in you, you've been going around with a hangdog look on your sour puss. And all the while you're so busy pining for that girl, you can hardly get your chores done. Hell, you're walking into walls like you're a damned zombie, Bolt."

"I didn't know it showed." Bolt grinned. He raised the hammer and then drove a nail straight into the board he had set in place.

Tom was right about him pining for Laurette, but he wasn't about to admit it. He was so smitten by the beautiful French singer, he hadn't been able to think of anything else. Ever since the first minute he'd laid eyes on her when she'd floated out onto the stage at the Prairie Schooner, he had been totally awestruck by her. He'd spent all of his waking hours thinking about how he could see her again without patronizing Monte Calhoun's saloon. He had been caught up in a world of fantasy as he'd done his chores those four days, dreaming the grandiose dreams about how he could win Laurette's heart.

"It shows." Tom dropped his arms and ambled over to where Bolt was working. He glanced down at the short stack of lumber. "So, what in the hell are you trying to do?"

"I'm making the stage bigger. Even with your tiny pea-brain, you ought to be able to figure it out." Bolt picked up another nail and hammered it into place.

"Why are you making it bigger? We built that stage when them Morningstar gals were staying here, but we don't even have a singer now, so what's the point?" Tom scratched his head, a puzzled look on his face. "Oh, no, Bolt. You're not going to . . . you're not even thinking it."

"Yes, I am," Bolt said with a sly look. He stood up and patted the new boards at the edge of the platform. "Miss Laurette Armand is going to sing from this very stage," he announced proudly.

Tom shook his head. "And does Miss Armand know it yet?"

"Not yet." Bolt grinned. "But she will soon enough. Now, how about giving me a hand?"

Harmony Sanchez entered the front door, carrying a basket of freshly gathered eggs in her hand. She looked over at the two men. "Oh, there you are, Bolt. I've been looking for you," she said as she walked over to him. "What's all the racket?"

Harmony wore a bib apron over her long-skirted, high-necked dress, but neither the apron nor the dress itself could hide the contour of her full breasts that pushed against the fabric. She wore no makeup and her long blonde hair hung in loose curls about her pretty face. When the bordello opened for business that evening, Harmony, as usual, would be wearing rouge and lipstick in her role as madam. She would also be wearing one of her sexy, revealing gowns.

Bolt had come across Harmony nearly a year ago, on the same day he had bought this ranch. She had been badly beaten and left to die on the open prairie between San Antonio and the Rocking Bar Ranch in Cow Town. She was unconscious when Bolt discovered her in the high grasses of the prairie and he had taken her to a doctor in San Antonio. After the doctor did what he could for her, Bolt took Harmony to his newly purchased ranch and nursed her back to health. When he found out that she didn't have any place to go, he offered her a job and a place to live and she had gratefully accepted both offers.

"Bolt's got it in his mind that he's gonna hire a singer to entertain the customers," Tom complained to Harmony. He sighed and shook his head.

"Don't be so grumpy, Tom," Harmony said cheerfully. "I think that's a good idea. The men will love it. I hope you find someone pretty, Bolt."

"Oh, she's pretty all right," Tom said with a big grin. "Present company excluded, she's the purtiest gal this side of Philadelphia."

"Oh, you've already hired her, then? Well, I hope she isn't all that pretty," Harmony said with a teasing lilt to her voice. She batted her eyes coyly at Bolt and fluffed her hair for his benefit.

Bolt felt suddenly uncomfortable. Thoughts of the beautiful, sensual, French singer, Laurette Armand, filled his mind and now he had been painfully reminded that he had a relationship with Harmony that involved more than her keeping house for him. Although Bolt had a self-imposed rule about never sleeping with the harlots who worked for him, he often took Harmony to his bed. She was the madam, not one of the harlots.

He knew that Harmony was in love with him and he loved her, too, he guessed, in his own way. She teased him sometimes about marrying her, but she never pushed it. She had graciously accepted the fact that he was not ready to settle down and maybe never would be. Harmony came to his bed willingly, knowing full well that he saw other women when he was away from the ranch. But the situation he was now creating for himself could become mighty awkward, he thought.

No, he couldn't do that to Harmony. Not in her own domicile. His bubble burst and he came to his senses when he realized that he wouldn't feel right about making passes at Laurette right under Harmony's nose. He had already spent many hours fantasizing about how he could be discreet with

Laurette, but he now knew that that's all it was. A fantasy. The state of euphoria that had engulfed him for the past four days slowly faded away. Oh, well, he hadn't approached Laurette yet about singing in his bordello. And, maybe he still would after all. She would be good for business and it would give him a great deal of satisfaction to steal her away from Monte Calhoun.

"No, I haven't hired her yet," he said as he picked up another board and set it in place. "You were looking for me, Harmony?" He glanced up at her.

"Yes. I wanted to ask you if it was all right if I was gone for a week or two. I wanted to visit my ailing aunt in Fredericksburg." Still clutching the basket of eggs in one hand, Harmony planted her hands on her hips and looked down at Bolt, a playful smile on her lips. "Now I'm not so sure I want to leave."

Bolt straightened up then and flexed his stiff shoulder muscles. "Go ahead and go. You don't need my permission," he said with an easy smile. And then his expression turned serious. "I know you've been worried about your aunt since you got the news of her illness. I think you should be with her."

"I do, too," Harmony said quietly as she lowered her arms. "From what Mrs. Johnson said in her letter, I don't think Aunt Bessie is going to live much longer. She's the only kin I've got left."

"She needs you, Harmony."

"I know she does, but I just don't like to leave you in a bind here."

"Just go, and don't worry your pretty little head about things here." Bolt put his arm around

Harmony and gave her a squeeze. "We'll manage. Not very well, but we'll manage," he said with that crooked little grin of his.

"The girls said they'd help you while I was gone," Harmony said. "They'll cook for you and keep your house in order until I get back."

"Good," said Tom. "As long as I don't have to eat Bolt's cooking, you have my permission to go."

"Thanks a lot, Tom. I'll miss you, too." Harmony smiled at Tom, then turned to Bolt. "I checked the stage schedule when I was in town yesterday. There's a stagecoach that leaves San Antonio at ten in the morning and I think I'll plan to be on it."

"Good enough," Bolt said. "I'll take you to town in the buggy in the morning and see you off."

The stagecoach was late.

Bolt fished his gold watch out of his pocket and checked the time for the fifth time that morning. He shook his head and tucked the watch back inside the small pocket in his trousers. He continued to pace back and forth in front of the stagecoach office, his boots clanking on the wooden planks of the boardwalk. Then he stepped out into the dusty street and looked for signs of the stagecoach. He'd done that at least five times, too.

It was eleven-thirty already and he was restless. Bolt didn't have an appointment, but he had decided to go to the Alamo Hotel where Miss Armand was staying and offer her a job as a singer at his bordello and he was anxious to get on with it. He just couldn't stand the thought of Laurette working for that bastard, Monte Calhoun.

Harmony Sanchez sat on a hard bench in front of the stagecoach stop, her neatly packed carpetbag at her feet. A folded coat was draped over her bag. She wore a comfortable traveling dress, light brown so it wouldn't show the trail dust, and shoes that were loose enough that they wouldn't pinch her toes. Her long blonde hair was pulled back away from her face and hung in tight curls at the back of her head. The small brown hat that perched on top of her head hid the ribbon that held her hair in place. Her stagecoach ticket was safely tucked inside the pocketbook that rested in her lap. The purse also contained the cash she would need for the trip, a hairbrush, a lace handkerchief, rouge, a pencil and writing tablet, and a few other personal items. She showed no signs of impatience as she watched Bolt pace along the boardwalk.

"You want to tell me about her?" Harmony finally asked as Bolt passed in front of her.

Bolt paused and gave her a puzzled look. "Who? What in the hell are you talking about?"

"The girl you're going to hire to sing at the bordello. That's what's on your mind, isn't it?" Harmony spoke as a friend with no hint of jealousy in her voice.

"Yeah, I guess it is." Bolt smiled dumbly. He walked over and sat down next to her. He leaned forward, his knees spread apart, and let his arms rest on his legs. He stared down at the weathered planks of the boardwalk as the images of Laurette flooded back into his mind. When he thought about Monte Calhoun, his blood began to boil.

"It's that new French singer at the Prairie Schooner, isn't it?" Harmony asked when Bolt didn't offer her any further information. "Miss Laurette Armand."

"Yeah, how'd you know?"

"It's not hard to figure out, Bolt." She reached over and patted his leg. "You and Tom came home all banged up the other night after you got into a fight with Monte Calhoun at the Prairie Schooner. I know how much you dislike Monte, so I was surprised you went in his saloon in the first place." She paused and looked into Bolt's eyes. "And, I saw the flyers when I was in town yesterday."

"Well, I wasn't trying to keep it a secret," Bolt said defensively. "I just wasn't sure I wanted to hire Miss Armand. But I think she'll be good for business."

"Yes, I think so, too. Some of the customers get impatient when they have to wait too long for one of the girls and the good Lord knows they can tolerate only so much of my piano playing while they're waiting." She laughed.

"Don't kid yourself, Harmony. All the men love you. Let me tell you, if you were one of the soiled doves, they'd all be waiting in your line."

"Why, thank you, Jared Bolt. Sometimes you can be downright sweet."

"Well, it's true." He leaned forward and looked up the street.

"Is she as pretty as her picture?"

Still leaning forward, Bolt turned his head and grinned at Harmony. "Prettier."

"Is she really?"

"Oh, much prettier. And she sings like an angel,"

Bolt said with an exaggerated sigh as he gazed up at the sky.

"Oh, really?" Harmony said sarcastically. "Now I know why you're so anxious to get rid of me." She picked up her pocketbook and drew it back as if to hit him with it.

Bolt ducked away. "You're not jealous, are you, Harmony?" he teased.

"Maybe, just a little," she pouted.

Bolt heard the loud rumbling of wagon wheels and looked up in time to see the stagecoach careening around the corner and into view. "Well, here's your buggy ride," he said as he stood up and picked up her coat and her carpetbag.

"Lucky for you," Harmony said as she stood up. "You were just about to get your teeth knocked down your throat."

"Why, Miss Harmony, you surprise me," he teased. "A sweet thing like you. You wouldn't do that to me, would you?"

"It's a good thing for you, you won't have to find out."

The stagecoach rolled to a clattering stop in front of the stage stop. The hulk of the coach rocked back and forth, its rusty springs moaning under the shifting weight, and then finally settled down on its frame as clouds of gritty dust spewed up around the wagon wheels. A young woman's face appeared at the dust-laden window of the coach as the curious passenger looked out.

Bolt and Harmony waited until the dust had settled before they walked over to the stagecoach. Bolt draped Harmony's coat over his arm and set the carpetbag down on the edge of the boardwalk.

"Sorry I'm late," said the short, stubby, Irish stage driver as he hopped down from the driver's seat. He tipped his top hat to them, then walked around and opened the door of the coach. He stuck his head inside. "You can step out and stretch your legs for a bit," he said to the passengers, "but we won't tarry here long, so don't you be wanderin' off."

The driver reached for Harmony's carpetbag. "Top o' the mornin' to ya. This all the luggage you'd be carryin'?"

"Yes," Harmony nodded. "I'll keep my coat with me." She reached over and took her coat from Bolt, draped it over her own arm.

The driver carried her piece of luggage around to the back of the coach where he scrambled up the ladder to tie it in place with the other bags.

A young, neatly dressed man emerged from the stagecoach, then turned and offered his hand to the young lady who had been looking out the window. The woman stepped down and looked around, then brushed the trail dust from her long, earth-colored skirt. The couple nodded politely to Bolt and Harmony and then walked a few feet away where they flexed their legs and their stiff backs.

"We'll be ready to roll as soon as I check with the stage clerk," the driver said to Harmony a few minutes later. He tipped his hat again. "Time to climb aboard," he called to the young couple as he headed toward the building.

Bolt took Harmony's arm and pulled her aside so the other two passengers could board. "Good-bye, Harmony," he said. "I hope you have a good trip."

Harmony reached over and took Bolt's hand in her own. "Bolt, I really do hope you can get Miss Armand to come to work for us," she said softly as she looked into his eyes. "Business has fallen off the past few days and those fellows who do ride out to our place aren't showing up until almost midnight."

"I've noticed that," Bolt said. "The men are spending their time at the Prairie Schooner instead of riding out to our place. If Monte decided to force Miss Armand to sing throughout the night, those randy fellows would never leave that blamed saloon."

The woman passenger smiled and nodded to Harmony as she passed by on her way to the stagecoach door, already hiking up the front of her long, full skirt so she could climb up onto the step.

Harmony returned the friendly gesture, then turned her attention back to Bolt. "Monte Calhoun could put us out of business if he was smart, couldn't he?" she asked.

"He's not that smart, Harmony, but don't you worry about it while you're gone. You'll have enough to think about with your Aunt Bessie. I hope she's better by the time you get there."

"I hope so, too." Harmony sighed. "Oh, Bolt, I'm going to miss you so much."

Bolt saw the tears in her eyes. He kissed her briefly on the lips then took her in his arms and held her tight. "Good-bye, Harmony," he whispered. "I'm going to miss you, too."

"Are you really?" She pulled away from him and looked up into his eyes, as if she were searching for some sign of reassurance.

"Of course I'll miss you, Harmony," he said with a serious look. "After all, there's nobody who can darn socks like you can."

Harmony glared at him for a moment, and drew back her pocketbook as if she was going to hit him with it. Changing her mind, she tossed her head back and smiled haughtily.

"Darning socks is a wife's job, Bolt. Maybe you'd better think about that while I'm gone."

CHAPTER SEVEN

Bolt was relieved when the stagecoach finally rolled away from the station. He waved a final goodbye and was glad that Harmony would have company on the long trip. He sighed and started up the street toward the Alamo Hotel, leaving his horse and buggy tied up near the stagecoach stop.

The sense of apprehension that had caused him to be fidgety all morning settled back into the pit of his stomach as he walked along the busy boardwalk. He knew that Monte Calhoun would stir up trouble if Miss Armand decided to switch to the Rocking Bar, but that wasn't what made Bolt edgy. He wasn't afraid of Calhoun. It was the fact that he was uneasy about calling on Laurette. He hadn't seen her since her opening night at the Prairie Schooner and he wasn't sure she would even talk to him.

He felt like an awkward young schoolboy courting a girl for the very first time and that fear of rejection continued to tug at him, as it had done for the past few days whenever he thought about facing

Laurette. That was why he was so nervous, he knew, and he had to keep reminding himself that he was going to see Miss Armand for the purpose of offering her a job. If she turned him down, then he shouldn't take it personally, should he?

Damn, those deep blue eyes of hers still haunted him. And her beautiful, sensual smile. He felt his knees go weak on him as he neared the Alamo Hotel and he hoped he didn't make a blithering fool of himself when he saw her again.

The pleasant aroma of baking bread and pastries assaulted Bolt's nostrils when he stepped inside the busy lobby of the hotel. He glanced at the Seth Thomas clock on the wall and saw that it was almost noon. His roiling stomach suddenly reminded him that he hadn't bothered to eat breakfast that morning.

Besides the three old-timers who lived at the hotel and spent most of their days sitting in the lobby watching the people come and go, there were a few people sitting in the plush chairs who looked like they might be waiting for someone to join them for lunch. Another small group, two men dressed in business suits and two women who wore hats and pretty daytime frocks, were already headed down the short hallway that led to the fancy hotel dining room, a favorite eating place among the townspeople.

Bolt wished now that he had invited Laurette to dine with him. If she didn't slam the door in his face, maybe he still would. She might be more inclined to listen to his offer in the pleasant surroundings of the dining room.

"Good morning, Charlie," he said as he stopped at the desk clerk's counter. He was familiar with the hotel and people who worked there.

The young clerk brushed away the lock of dark hair that hung down in his face and looked up from his paperwork.

"Well, howdy, Bolt. How are you today?" Charlie said, a boyish grin spreading across his face.

"Just fine. Can you tell me which room Miss Armand occupies?"

"I sure can," Charlie said with a sly grin and a knowing nod of the head. "She sure is purty, ain't she?"

Bolt wanted to punch the young clerk in the mouth for that suggestive look he gave him, which indicated that Bolt was a lecherous old fool. But that's the way Charlie was. As desk clerk at the popular hotel, Charlie enjoyed being in the position where he could keep track of the people who passed through the lobby. Although the young, awkwardly dressed lad seemed to get some sexual satisfaction from imagining what went on behind closed doors, Bolt doubted that he had ever known the pleasures of taking a woman to his bed.

"What room is she in?" he asked.

"I'm the luckiest jasper in San Antonio, Bolt. You know why?"

"Why, Charlie?" Bolt didn't really give a damn. Charlie was harmless enough, though, and since he'd done a few favors for Bolt in the past, Bolt tolerated the clerk's need to brag and gossip.

"'Cause all the fellows want to get close to Laurette, if you know what I mean, and I'm the only one she'll talk to. Yessir, she comes by my desk seven or eight times a day and she always speaks to me. Hell, I'm the envy of every man in town." Charlie smiled obscenely, exposing the dark gap in his mouth where his two front teeth were missing. His missing teeth and his mismatched, forever rumpled clothing were enough to make him seem like a simpleminded fool, but the way the locks of his greasy hair always hung in his face made him look like the town idiot.

Bolt gritted his teeth and shifted his weight to the other foot.

"Her room number, Charlie," he said again.

"Yes, of course. I don't blame you for being in a hurry. Miss Armand is in room one-eighteen. Down the hall, last room on the left." Charlie pointed to the hallway that was on the opposite side of the lobby from the hall that led to the dining room.

"Thanks, Charlie."

When Bolt found the room, he stopped in front of the door and listened. He didn't hear any noise inside the room and hoped Miss Armand wasn't sleeping. He glanced down at his clothing, brushed a piece of lint from his trousers, straightened the collar of his clean, white shirt. He removed his hat, held it in his hand, then rapped lightly on the door.

"Just a minute," Laurette called from inside.

The sound of her musical voice brought back the images of her beauty full-blown in Bolt's mind and he felt all giddy inside when he thought about her haunting blue eyes.

Soon he heard the soft padding of footsteps in the room and then the metal clink of the doorknob as it turned. The door swung open and Laurette Armand stood in front of him, even more beautiful than he remembered her. She looked surprised to see him.

Laurette wore a bright blue dress that exactly matched the color of her eyes. The gown was proper for daytime wear with its high collar and the long, full skirt that was fluffed out by the layers of petticoats beneath it. The gingham dress buttoned up the front and clung softly to her full, rounded bosom, accentuating her slim waistline. Her only jewelry was a white cameo pendant that hung from a delicate gold chain around her neck.

Her long raven hair hung in soft curls about her face. Her lips were ruby red, sensually moist, and she wore just a hint of rouge on her cheeks.

Bolt was struck speechless by her beauty. The delicate scent of her perfume filled his nostrils and, as he breathed it in, he felt like his legs would go out from under him. No woman had affected him quite that way before. He opened his mouth to speak, but nothing came out.

"Oh, *Monsieur* Bolt," Laurette exclaimed, her eyes wide. I . . . I was expecting someone else."

"You look lovely today, Miss Laurette . . . er, Miss Armand," he stammered, not able to take his eyes off of her beautiful eyes.

"Merci, Monsieur Bolt." She smiled demurely.

"Would you care to have lunch with me, Miss Armand?" he blurted out. Nervous, he fiddled with the Stetson he held in both hands, rotating it slowly with his fingers.

"Oh, I am so sorry, *Monsieur* Bolt. I have already accepted an invitation to dine with *Monsieur*

Calhoun. He should be here in just a few minutes."

Bolt cursed under his breath. So Monte was courting Laurette. Well, Calhoun was the last person in the world he wanted to see just then, especially since he wanted to talk business with Laurette.

"Maybe I should come back another time," he suggested.

"What is it you wanted?"

"Miss Armand, I have an offer to make you concerning your singing. Could you spare a couple of minutes to talk to me?"

"Yes. Please come in." She moved aside to let Bolt enter her room. She left the door wide open after he stepped inside.

He saw that she had added some of her own personal touches to the room so that it was more feminine than the normal austere hotel room. A writing desk had been added to one corner of the room and there was a small love seat against one wall. A bright, colorful afghan was draped over the love seat. Several paintings hung on the walls and the bed was covered with a pink, fluffy comforter. The whole room smelled like the heady, flowery scent he had now come to associate with Laurette.

"Please sit down," she offered.

"No thanks. I won't be here that long. Miss Armand, I would like you to come and sing at my place. I'll pay you twice as much as Monte Calhoun is paying you."

Laurette's eyebrows pinched to a frown and then she smiled. "Who would I sing for? Your cows? Or would it be just for your own personal entertainment?"

"Miss Armand, I run a bordello out at my ranch and I'd like you to sing for the customers in the large parlor where there is a bar and a small stage."

A stunned look came over Laurette's face. "Then you are a . . . a . . . what *Monsieur* Calhoun called you the other night."

"No, I'm not a pimp. I run a bordello and the girls who work for me have chosen their own profession. They're nice, decent girls."

"How could you consider them decent if they let the men do terrible things to them?"

"Men have normal needs and the harlots satisfy those needs," Bolt said. "It's better than having those men raping innocent women."

"No, *Monsieur* Bolt. I won't sing for such vulgar men."

"You're already singing for them," Bolt said. "Some of the men who go to the Prairie Schooner are the same men who patronize my bordello. Tell me, do you like working at the Prairie Schooner?"

Laurette turned away from him briefly and then looked directly at him. "No, I really don't like working at the Prairie Schooner," she said. "The men are too noisy, too crude. And I don't care for *Monsieur* Calhoun. He has become too demanding."

"In what way?" Bolt asked.

"He now makes us work long hours for the same pay and he forces Cherie and me to mingle with the customers when we're not on stage. Some of the men get very drunk. They say vulgar things to us and they try to maul us with their filthy hands." Laurette shuddered. She walked over to her dressing table, picked up a blue hat and positioned it on her head, fastening it in place with a pearl-studded hat pin. "I'm pretty tough and I can hold my own with a man," she said, glancing at Bolt's reflection in the mirror, "but poor Cherie, she breaks into tears sometimes. It hurts me to see her so shamed."

"What about Ken Selves?" Bolt asked, incensed that the women were being treated so badly. "You said he was so brave. You said he would protect you. Why doesn't he stand up for you?"

"Ken would defend my honor in a minute, but I won't let him fight my battles. It is *Monsieur* Calhoun's place to see that Cherie and I are not molested while we are working at the Prairie Schooner, but he does nothing about it."

"That doesn't surprise me."

After a final check in the mirror to be sure her hat was in place, Laurette turned to face Bolt. "It is very humiliating to be treated like a hussy, *Monsieur* Bolt. But you are a man and I don't expect you to understand."

"I do understand, Miss Armand," Bolt said. "That is why I insist that the girls who work for me are treated with respect. If any fellow gets drunk or if he gets rough with one of the girls, he's booted out and forbidden to return to the bordello."

Laurette looked at him long and hard, as if she were trying to figure him out. "It isn't only the customers of the Prairie Schooner who bother me. It's *Monsieur* Calhoun, too. He is constantly trying to press his attentions on me. In fact, he told me last night that if I didn't give in to his advances, he would fire me."

"Is that why you're having lunch with him today?" The words came out more sarcastically than Bolt had wanted, but he couldn't understand why Laurette would consent to dine with Calhoun if she detested him so much. He didn't know why a woman as beautiful as Laurette felt that she had to give in to Calhoun's demands.

"No. Monte thinks so, I'm sure, but I wanted to talk to him to see if he would change his ways and I thought it would be best to do it in a public place. I certainly don't want to be alone with the man."

Bolt saw her shudder. "Are you afraid of him?" he asked.

"A little, I guess," Laurette said as she looked down.

"Has he ever hurt you?"

She shook her head and looked up at Bolt. "No, Monte has never hurt me. Nor has he ever threatened to hurt me. But I've heard rumors that he's been cruel to women on several occasions."

"I've heard that, too," Bolt said.

"I think he knows better than to get rough with me," Laurette said with confidence, "but still, I know from my own observations of him that Monte has a violent temper when he's provoked. Just like that night he attacked you."

"And he's easily provoked," Bolt said as he rubbed his chin, which was still sore from the fight.

"That's why I want to talk to him in the hotel dining room where there will be other people around. I want him to know that his demands have become intolerable."

"Monte Calhoun won't change," Bolt said.

"Maybe not, but quite frankly, *Monsieur* Bolt, I need the money."

"Then, why don't you come to work for me?" Bolt said. "I'll pay you double whatever Monte is paying you and I'll guarantee you that my customers won't bother you or Cherie."

"You would do that?" Laurette said, her blue eyes full of awe.

"Yes, of course. What is Calhoun paying you?"

"He pays me twenty-five dollars a week."

"Then I'll pay you fifty," said Bolt without hesitation.

"Ken and Cherie would have to come with me," Laurette said. "I'm responsible for them."

"Of course. I include Ken and Cherie in my offer." Bolt smiled. "I'll pay them more money than they're making at the Prairie Schooner."

"Ken makes a mere pittance. Plus all the free drinks he can drink," she added with a bitter laugh. "Ken doesn't even drink liquor and Monte knew that when he made Ken the offer."

Bolt shook his head, not surprised by Calhoun's swindling tactics. "I'll pay both Ken and Cherie a decent salary."

"Cherie is my personal maid," Laurette said. "She is very shy and she doesn't want to perform on the stage in front of those men. Especially in that short little frock *Monsieur* Calhoun makes her wear."

"I understand. We don't need Cherie to perform at the bordello. She can be just your maid and if you'd prefer to pay her out of your own earnings, I'll give you an additional amount for that purpose."

"Where is your . . . your ranch, *Monsieur* Bolt? Is it close?"

"The Rocking Bar Ranch is two miles south of San Antonio," Bolt said. "Not a far piece, but I wouldn't want you riding back into town late at night. I'll provide you and Cherie with separate living quarters. You can each have one of the little cottages until we can finish off a bigger cabin for the two of you to live in. Ken Selves can stay in the bunkhouse with my two cowhands. We can partition off part of the bunkhouse so he can have his privacy."

With her hands folded and held at her waistline, Laurette looked at him for such a long time that Bolt became uncomfortable under her piercing stare. He wanted to glance away and catch his breath, even if it was only for an instant. But he couldn't. Her haunting beauty held him under its hypnotic spell.

Finally Laurette sighed and stared down at the braided rug as she walked away from him. She stood at the window a minute, pulled the curtain aside and stared out at the tree-dotted field behind the hotel. And then, as if she'd come to some decision, she whirled around and walked back over to him.

"*Monsieur* Bolt, there is something about your face that tells me that I can trust you," she said. "Perhaps it is your stark blue eyes, or perhaps it is the fact that you aren't afraid to look me in the eye."

She paused and the silence was awkward.

"Thank you," Bolt said, feeling a need to fill the void and not knowing what else to say.

"You have made me a very generous offer and I would very much like to accept it, but . . ."

Bolt's heart sank.

"But," Laurette continued, "I just would not feel comfortable working in a house of ill repute."

"You would not be singing in the same building where the girls . . . uh . . . perform their services," Bolt said. "You would be singing in a room that is both a parlor and a bar. Tom and I will be there to see that everything runs smoothly for you."

"But still, I don't wish to associate with . . . with soiled doves."

"I'll tell you what, Miss Armand, you come out to my place and meet the girls who work for me. Then, if you don't want to stay there and sing at my bordello, I'll bring you back into town and still pay you a full week's salary."

Laurette smiled. "You make it very hard to turn down your offer, *Monsieur* Bolt. Although I think you're quite bold to ask me to sing at your . . . your house of pleasure, I will do it. I don't think I could face another night at the Prairie Schooner."

"Good," Bolt smiled. "And please call me just Bolt."

"If you'll call me Laurie." She laughed.

"I'd like that, Laurie."

"I'll tell *Monsieur* Calhoun of my decision during lunch."

"He won't like it."

"I know, and I don't want to stay here in town and face his wrath." Laurette sighed. Again she stared at the braided rug. "Bolt, do you think it would be possible for us to make the move to your place this afternoon?"

"Yes, of course," Bolt said. "I brought the carriage to town this morning, so I can take you all back with me. Your pay will begin today, but I won't expect you to work tonight. I want you to rest up. Tomorrow's Friday and we'll have a grand opening party for you tomorrow night, if that's not too soon."

"Tomorrow night would be fine," she smiled. "That's very kind of you. You don't know how much I would like to have a day to rest."

"You'll have every Sunday off, too. We don't open the bordello on Sundays."

"You are much fairer than *Monsieur* Calhoun. He insisted that I work every night. He said that I would have plenty of time to rest during the day."

Bolt shook his head. "He would wear you out in less than a month."

"I think so." Laurette smiled. "We can be ready to go in a couple of hours. Could you come back for us then?"

"Yes." He tugged his watch out of his pocket and saw that it was a little after noon. "I'll be back for you about two o'clock."

"We'll be ready to go," Laurette said.

"And now I want to get out of here before Calhoun shows up to take you to lunch," Bolt said as he tucked his gold watch back in his pocket.

"I wish you could be with me when I inform Monte that I'll no longer be working at the Prairie Schooner," Laurette said. She looked at Bolt, her eyes full of apprehension.

"You'll do all right, Laurette. You're a strong woman. And don't worry, Calhoun wouldn't dare strike you in public," he said lightheartedly. "His pride wouldn't let him."

"I know," she said with an uneasy smile. "It's just that I'm dreading this meeting with Monte. He'll be angry."

"Yes, he'll be madder than a trapped rat, but he won't hit you. For now it's best that he doesn't see the two of us together. There's no sense in adding fuel to his fury."

"You're right." Laurette laughed. "I'm afraid Monte doesn't like you and if he saw us together, that would send him into a fierce rage. I'll have to face him alone."

Bolt slipped his hat on his head, squared it up. "Then I'll bid you good-bye for now, Laurie. I'll be back to fetch you at two."

"Good-bye, Bolt."

Bolt turned to leave Laurette's hotel room and already knew he was too late to avoid a face-to-face confrontation with Monte Calhoun when he heard the heavy footsteps coming down the hall.

CHAPTER EIGHT

Bolt stepped out into the hallway just as Monte Calhoun approached Miss Armand's room. The two men were not more than five feet apart.

Calhoun was all gussied up in a brown suit that looked brand-new and made him appear like a successful businessman. The suit included a vest, which covered a white shirt. Monte wore a red string tie and his cowboy boots, and carried his brown, stained Stetson in his hand. Bolt figured Monte had just come from the barbershop because his slicked-back hair was neatly trimmed.

Calhoun's eyes went wide with surprise when he spotted Bolt coming out of Laurette's hotel room. His jaw went slack, his mouth fell open. After the original shock wore off, Monte's cheeks flushed with anger.

"What in the hell are you doing here, you slimy, sneaky bastard?" Calhoun shouted as he rushed up to Bolt.

"Good afternoon," Bolt said politely. He sidestepped around Calhoun and started to leave.

Monte grabbed his shoulder and dug his fingers into the flesh. "I said, what're you doing coming out of Laurette's room?" he asked gruffly.

Laurette appeared in the doorway. "Please, Monte, don't cause trouble here," she said.

Calhoun turned to look at Laurette. "Why'd you let this dirty bastard into your room?" he demanded as he shook Bolt's shoulder. "Did he force his way in? I'll kill him."

"No, he didn't force his way in," she said. "I'll explain later."

Bolt jerked his shoulder away from Monte's clutches and straightened his shirt. "Good-bye, Laurie," he called, and then headed up the hallway toward the hotel lobby.

Fuming mad, Calhoun looked at Bolt's back as Bolt walked away from him. He glanced at Laurette, his cold eyes full of accusation, then he looked at Bolt again, as if trying to decide whether or not to go after the man.

"Why'd he call you Laurie?" he asked, his voice crackling with anger.

"That's what all my friends call me," Laurette answered simply.

"You never told me to call you Laurie."

"You've never been a friend, Monte," Laurette said softly.

"What was that disreputable bastard doing in your room, Laurette? Don't you know what he is?" The color in Calhoun's cheeks deepened with rage as he stood in the hallway outside Miss Armand's room. He was so angry he nearly choked as he spoke.

"He was talking to me, that's all."

"You open the door for that low-down skunk and yet I've never been invited into your room?" Calhoun roared.

"No, you haven't," Laurette said.

"What'd he want?" Calhoun demanded.

"I had planned to tell you over lunch."

"You'll tell me now, lady."

"If you insist," Laurette said from the doorway. "Bolt asked me to come to work for him. He wants me to sing at his place."

"Why, the nerve of that stupid, sneaky bastard," Calhoun said as he glanced up the empty corridor. "You mean Bolt was foolish enough to think that you'd actually consider it? Oh, that poor, dumb sonofabitch." He laughed uproariously, slapping his knee.

"Monte, I accepted Bolt's offer."

"You what?" Calhoun's laughter stopped abruptly. His head jerked up and his eyes narrowed as he glared at Laurette suspiciously.

"I'm going to work for Bolt."

"But you can't."

"Yes, I can, Monte," Laurette said firmly. Calhoun had a way of intimidating her with his demanding voice and she wasn't going to let him do it this time.

"But you work for me, Laurette."

"Not anymore, Monte. Bolt made me a better

offer than you did." She kept her voice even and calm because she didn't want to upset Calhoun any more than he already was. She'd witnessed Monte's violent temper more than once and, although it hadn't been directed at her before, she didn't trust him.

"You can't do this to me, Laurette," Calhoun said in a loud, dogmatic voice as he struggled to control his anger. "You can't quit the Prairie Schooner just like that."

"I already have, *Monsieur* Calhoun. I won't work for you any longer."

"But what about me?" Calhoun whined. "What about my saloon. I need you there, pretty lady. You're drawing the customers in like I've never seen before. What'll I do if you leave?"

"You should have thought about that when I asked for one day off a week for me and Cherie and Ken. You should have thought about that when you made us work long into the night."

"But that's what the customers wanted. You know damned well they want you up there on that stage," Calhoun said, trying to reason with her.

"Then you should have paid us more if you expected us to work until the wee hours of the morning."

Calhoun's face twisted to an ugly snarl. "You're a nobody from New Orleans who thinks your shit doesn't stink. You aren't worth more money, Laurette," he said sarcastically.

"Maybe not, but I wouldn't work for you for any amount of money," she said, her own sarcasm bubbling to the surface. "Bolt was right the other night when he said you didn't know how to treat a lady."

"Why, you haughty little bitch!" he yelled. "You ought to have your face slapped." He drew back an open hand as if to strike her.

Although her instinct was to duck, Laurette didn't flinch except to blink her eyes. Inside, she was trembling, but she just stood there and watched him. She wouldn't give him the satisfaction of knowing that he was frightening her.

Calhoun dropped his hand. "Go ahead and quit, Laurette. I don't really care," he said with a shrug of his shoulders. "I'll just make Cherie my star. The fellows who come to the Prairie Schooner think she's just as pretty and voluptuous as you are anyway. I'll buy her a whole new wardrobe of sexy outfits and she'll have everyone drooling at her feet."

Laurette cringed at the thought. She noticed the way Monte was changing tactics in an effort to get her to stay at the Prairie Schooner. He vacillated between begging her to stay and telling her he didn't need her. It was all an act and none of it would work with her. She had learned all about his deceptive ways.

"Cherie doesn't want to perform on stage and you know it," she said. "She hates wearing that scanty little costume you make her wear, and she hates the way you use her to tease the men. You've made her feel like a cheap hussy. Cherie Bonwit is coming with me. So is Ken Selves."

"You can have Ken. I don't like that little wimp

anyway. And we'll see about Cherie. She might have ideas of her own."

"She does have ideas of her own. That's why she is coming with me."

"Have you told Cherie that you're going to whisk her off to perform at that evil house of sin?" Calhoun said with an arrogant sneer.

"That's none of your concern," Laurette said defiantly. "Cherie is my personal maid and my very best friend. Nothing more."

Monte Calhoun looked beyond Laurette for a moment and glanced into her room. Then he stared down at the hat he held in his hands, deep in thought.

"I don't understand why you're doing this to me, Laurette," he said quietly as he stood there looking like a whipped dog. "I need you to sing at the Prairie Schooner. Why are you leaving me?"

Laurette was not fooled by this sudden show of gentle desperation. It was another of Monte's ploys to get her to stay on at the Prairie Schooner.

"The main reason I'm leaving you is that you allowed your drunken, rowdy customers to manhandle me and Cherie while we were working," she said. "It was very humiliating to both of us."

"Dammit, that's what you were getting paid for," he protested.

"No, Monte. I was getting paid to sing."

Calhoun's sudden smile was condescending. "Well, if that's all that's bothering you," he said with an exaggerated tone of cheerfulness in his voice, "then, I'll just keep the rowdy customers away from you and Cherie."

Laurette sighed. "It's not just that, Monte. You know what my grievances are."

"All right, then I'll pay you five dollars more a week and I'll guarantee you that you won't have to work past, say, one or two in the morning. And you can have your damned day off a week that you want."

"It's too late, Monte. I've already made my decision to work for Bolt, and nothing you can say will change my mind."

"Don't you know what you're getting yourself into?" Calhoun said, raising his voice again. "Bolt runs a house of prostitution, for godsakes. You'll be singing in a goddamned whorehouse."

"Bolt told me I'd be working in his bordello and I know full well what that is."

"You don't make any sense at all. You won't work at the Prairie Schooner because the men are too crude for you, and yet, you're willing to work in a goddamned whorehouse," Calhoun said, his voice shrill with accusation. "What kind of men do you think patronize whorehouses? Saints who wouldn't think of touching your precious body? Hell, no. I'll tell you who visits whorehouses. Vile, lustful men who will think of nothing else besides getting into your panties. That's why they go to whorehouses."

"I don't want to discuss it anymore," Laurette said hoping the flush of embarrassment that was creeping into her cheeks didn't show. "My mind is made up."

"But you're making a terrible mistake, Laurette,"

Calhoun persisted.

"I've made them before."

"You'll be associating with riff-raff," Calhoun said.

"It seems that I'm already doing that at the Prairie Schooner."

"Bolt will probably turn you into a whore."

"*Monsieur* Calhoun, if that's all you think of my character, then I think you have misjudged me. I will sing for the bold gentleman."

She stepped back and started to close the door, but Calhoun stuck his foot out.

"Wait a minute. What about lunch?" he asked as he withdrew his boot.

"No thank you, *Monsieur* Calhoun. I've lost my appetite."

Laurette saw the anger return to Monte's eyes.

"You filthy whore!" he yelled as he drew back his hand and doubled up his fist.

Laurette ducked back and slammed the door in his face, quickly bolting the latch.

"You bitch!" he shouted as he slammed his fist against her door. "You'll be sorry about this, you dirty, whoring traitor!"

Laurette leaned against the locked door and held her breath as Calhoun's vengeful words echoed in her ears. She prayed silently that he wouldn't knock her door down and attack her.

Although it was only a matter of seconds, it seemed like a long, long time before she finally heard the heavy clanking of Monte's boots on the bare floor as he walked up the hall and away from her room.

As Calhoun's footsteps faded, she stepped away from the door and sighed with relief that he was gone. An involuntary shudder coursed through her body.

She knew that she hadn't seen the last of Monte Calhoun.

CHAPTER NINE

When Bolt heard Calhoun's foosteps coming down the hall, he quickly scooted across the lobby and sat down next to the three elderly gentlemen. He snatched up a newspaper from the low table next to the sofa and held it in front of his face, just low enough so that he could see over it. He had waited in the lobby, just around the corner from the long hall, in case Calhoun gave Laurette some trouble.

Charlie, the desk clerk, always hungry for a new tidbit of gossip, had wanted to leave his station and join Bolt at the corner wall, but Bolt had insisted that Charlie stay behind the counter.

Bolt had been too far away to hear the conversation between Laurette Armand and Monte Calhoun, but he'd heard Monte raise his voice a couple of times. And he'd heard Calhoun's final vicious outburst against Laurette and the loud slamming of the door. Not knowing at that point whether Calhoun was inside or outside of Laurette's room, he'd been prepared to dash down the hall to go to

Laurette's aid if necessary. The sound of the loud, determined footsteps a few seconds later told him that Calhoun was headed for the lobby.

Charlie heard the footsteps, too. Resting both hands on the counter, he leaned forward and, with no luck, he tried to peer around the corner and into the hallway.

A minute later, Monte Calhoun wheeled around the corner, his stained brown Stetson on his head, his arms swinging at his sides. His head was lowered and he stared down at the floor as he walked.

Bolt scooted down in the plush sofa a little more, raised the newspaper so that he could just barely see over it.

Calhoun glanced over at the curious desk clerk as he passed the counter.

"What in the hell are you staring at, mister?" he growled.

Charlie jumped back. "Oh, nothing, sir. Nothing at all. Just daydreaming," he said as he looked down at the counter and began shuffling some papers.

Calhoun's head dropped again and he stared down at the Oriental rug that covered the floor as he marched toward the door. He never looked around as he pushed the heavy oak door open and went outside. He slammed the door behind him.

Bolt remained on the sofa until he saw Calhoun pass by the window on his way to the Prairie Schooner. Calhoun was mad and Bolt knew that someone would catch the brunt of Monte's temper when it exploded. A man like that couldn't hold it in.

Satisfied that Calhoun was gone, Bolt got up and tossed the paper on the table. He made his way to

Laurette's room, ignoring Charlie's questions and comments as he passed the clerk's counter.

"I'll come with you, Bolt," Charlie said as he started to come around the counter.

"No, you stay there, Charlie."

"But, Miss Armand is a resident of this hotel and I'm responsible for her safety," Charlie insisted.

"She didn't call out for help. I'll take care of her."

Charlie went back behind the counter. "Oh, of course, I understand," he said with a lewd grin. "You want to be alone with the pretty lady."

Again, Bolt ignored Charlie's remark. He went on down the hall and rapped lightly on Laurette's door. "Laurie, it's me, Bolt," he called.

He heard the scraping of metal as Laurette slid the bolt open. The doorknob turned and she opened the door cautiously. When she saw that it was Bolt, she opened the door wide.

"It is you," she sighed. "Come in."

"Are you all right, Laurie?" he asked as he entered her room.

"Yes." Laurette pushed the door shut and stood beside him for a moment, her body trembling.

"Did Calhoun hurt you?" Bolt leaned forward and looked at her face for evidence of bruises. With the door closed, and with Laurette so close to him, he felt suddenly flushed, as if he'd been caught in a blast of hot air.

"No, he just scared me half to death," she said with a deep sigh of relief. "That man's got a violent temper."

"That's why I stuck around. I would have heard you if you had screamed."

"Where were you?" she asked as she removed her hat and walked over to set it on the dressing table. "I didn't see you."

"In the lobby. I wanted to make sure Calhoun didn't rough you up."

"That was very thoughtful of you, Bolt," she said as she strolled back over to face him. "You know, I think Monte actually would have struck me if I hadn't slammed the door in his face."

"He might have. There was no one around to see him do it."

Without warning, Laurette threw her arms around Bolt's neck and squeezed him. "Oh, Bolt, I'm so glad you're here," she cried. "I was so scared." She let her arms fall, then wrapped them around his slim waist and held on for dear life.

The delicate scent of her heady perfume drifted up to his nostrils as her warm, trembling body pressed against his. He put his arms around her shoulders and held her close, certain that Laurette didn't realize that her firm breasts were crushing against his chest. He hadn't realized how tall she was until she buried her head into the crook of his shoulder.

Laurette felt good in his arms. She was soft and pliable as she melted against him and he sensed an affectionate side to her nature that he hadn't noticed when she'd been on the stage at the Prairie Schooner. She smelled like a basketful of freshly cut flowers and although he had promised himself that he would stick to a business relationship with Miss Armand, he found himself already wanting to spend more time than he should with her.

"You're safe, Laurie," he said softly as she

burrowed deeper into his protective arms. "Nobody's going to hurt you."

As suddenly as she had come to him, she unlocked her arms from his waist and backed away. "Look at me. I'm making a fool of myself," she said with a weak smile as she dabbed at her tear-filled eyes.

"No, you're not, Laurie," Bolt said.

"I barely flinched when I thought Monte was going to hit me and, now that it's all over, I feel like I'm going to shake apart."

She held her hands up and Bolt saw that they were still quivering. He took both of her hands and cupped them in his.

"That's normal," he said.

Bolt squeezed her hands and, for a long moment, they gazed into each other's eyes. And then Laurette withdrew her hands and turned away, as if she were afraid of her own emotions. She walked over and opened her door, glanced out into the hall, then returned, leaving the door open this time.

"I'm grateful for your concern." Laurette looked at him and smiled. "Just knowing that you waited in the lobby makes me feel better."

"Are you sure you're all right, Laurie?"

"Yes. I just want to get out of here as soon as possible. As soon as Ken and Cherie return, we can get our things packed up and be ready to leave when you are."

"Where are Ken and Cherie?"

"They left a little while ago to eat at the small cafe down the street. On what Calhoun pays us, we can't afford to eat here at the hotel very often."

"Let's you and I go eat lunch in the hotel dining

room while we're waiting for them," Bolt suggested.

"But what if Monte is in there eating? I don't ever want to see that man again."

"He isn't there," Bolt assured her. "Monte's gone. I watched him storm out of the hotel and head for his saloon."

"But what if he comes back? He might try to cause trouble," Laurette said. "I'm worried about what he might do to you."

"After all that yelling he did in the hallway, I don't think Calhoun will show his face around here for a while."

"You heard us arguing?"

"Not really. I just heard his loud mouth." Bolt laughed. "Now, quit your worrying and let's go have some lunch." He offered her his arm.

Laurette whirled away from him without a word, without as much as a polite smile or a courteous "No thank you."

The cheerful smile faded from Bolt's lips. He was disappointed. Laurette seemed tender and affectionate one minute and then she seemed to turn cold and insensitive the next minute. It was as if she were afraid to let her feelings show, as if she didn't trust a man, or his motives.

His arm still crooked, Bolt watched numbly as Laurette walked over to her dressing table. She picked up her blue, feathered hat, leaned down so she could see her reflection in the mirror, and pinned the hat atop her head with the pearl-studded hat pin. When the hat was secure, she reached over and picked up a small bottle and opened it. Bolt could smell the perfume as she dabbed a little behind each ear and across the smooth flesh of her neck.

After she set the bottle down, she turned and smiled at Bolt, as if waiting for his approval. As she walked toward him, her bright blue eyes twinkled with a coy, teasing expression. Laurette was flirting with him, Bolt was sure of it.

"It would be my pleasure to dine with you, *Monsieur* Bolt," she said as she slipped her arm into his.

There were only a few customers in the saloon when Monte Calhoun marched back into the Prairie Schooner. Ox Jarboe was one of them. Jarboe was the only one who sat at the long bar.

Ox sat on a high stool, his hand wrapped around a tumbler full of beer. His old, battered hat sat on the bar. He wore a clean shirt and yesterday's rumpled trousers. He had scrubbed his bearded face and run a comb through his long, shaggy hair, and he looked as decent as he was going to look the rest of that day.

Jarboe was on his second beer and after Sam, the barkeep, served him one more, Ox would be ready to wander about town to see if anyone needed him to work for them for a few hours that afternoon. Jarboe didn't have a regular job and, when he wasn't busy with his get-rich-quick schemes, he did odd jobs around town to keep him in spending money.

Ox Jarboe had a little money set aside in case he wanted to invest in the Prairie Schooner, but he was going to wait a couple of weeks to make damned sure Calhoun could finally make a go of the saloon before he put his money on the line. So far, with

Laurette Armand there to draw in the customers, things looked promising for the Prairie Schooner. Business had increased tenfold since the French gal had begun singing there, but Ox had his reservations about Calhoun. Although he and Monte were good friends, he didn't trust Calhoun to make a success of anything. He knew that Calhoun didn't have a good business head on his shoulders or, if he did, his mean temper kept blowing it away.

"Are you back already?" Sam Norris asked from behind the bar as Calhoun stomped across the room looking like a ferocious bear.

Ox Jarboe turned and saw the angry expression on his friend's face as Calhoun marched up to the bar and shoved an empty bar stool out of his way.

"Give me a double shot of whiskey, Sam," Calhoun ordered as he slammed his hat down on the counter.

"What's the matter, Monte? Did they run out of food at the Alamo Hotel?" Jarboe said in a joking manner. "Or did Miss Armand stand you up?"

Usually, Ox could kid Monte out of a foul mood. He soon discovered that this wasn't one of those times. Sam set the double shot of whiskey in front of Monte and when Monte drank it all down in one gulp, Ox knew the problem was more serious than a mere temper tantrum on Calhoun's part. Monte could put the whiskey away at night, but he didn't usually drink during the day.

"That damned bitch quit on me," Calhoun snarled as he slid the empty tumbler across the counter for a refill.

"Quit what?" Sam asked as he poured more

whiskey into the glass.

"What in the hell do you think she quit?" Calhoun roared. "She quit her job."

"You mean Laurette ain't gonna be working here no more?" Jarboe asked, disconcerted by the news. His thick eyebrows squeezed together in a frown.

"That's what I said, ain't it?" Calhoun snapped, his nostrils flaring with his anger. He downed his second drink.

"Well, I'll be damned. How come she quit?" Jarboe asked, stroking his bushy beard as he looked over at Calhoun. His hopes for making an easy fortune by investing in the Prairie Schooner plummeted, although the fact that Laurette had quit didn't really surprise him. Monte treated the girl like a damned slave and then bellyached because she wouldn't give in to his persistent advances.

"You ain't gonna believe this, but Laurette is going to work for Bolt," Calhoun said.

"As a whore?" Jarboe asked.

"As a singer, she claims," Calhoun said in a mocking manner. "But, hell, you know damned well Bolt's gonna turn her into a whore once she gets out there to his place. I tried to tell her that bastard was a pimp."

Ox patted his friend on the shoulder. "Don't worry about it, Monte. Laurette is too refined for that. After a couple of days working in that whorehouse, she'll come crawling back to you, begging you to take her back."

"Bolt won't let her go. I know that bastard. Give me another drink, Sam."

"Drinking isn't going to solve your problems,

Monte," the short, balding barkeep said.

"I said give me a drink," Calhoun demanded. "I don't need your advice."

Sam shrugged his shoulders and filled the glass again.

Calhoun took only a healthy swig of the whiskey this time, then stared into the glass for a long time, lost in his bitter, sullen thoughts.

The drinks hit him hard. He hadn't bothered to eat breakfast that morning. Instead, he'd had a couple of stiff drinks at his house while he was getting ready for his first date with Laurette, and then he'd gone to the saloon and had another drink with Ox Jarboe while he was waiting until it was time to go to the hotel to meet Laurette.

"Ox, I want you to go with me," he said after a while.

"Where are we going?"

"We're going over to the hotel and get Laurette before she has a chance to go out to Bolt's place," he said with an evil sneer.

"You mean you're going to kidnap her?" Jarboe said as his head snapped back.

"Not exactly," Calhoun smiled. "I'm just going to bring Miss Armand over here where I can talk some sense into her."

"What're you gonna do, keep her here at the saloon day and night so she can't run off to Bolt's place?" Jarboe scoffed.

"That's the general idea, my friend," Calhoun said with a proud smirk, his speech slurred from the effects of the strong whiskey. "Laurette can sleep in one of the back rooms. We'll put a cot in there for her."

"I suppose you'll hire a guard to see that she stays there," Jarboe said sarcastically.

"That's a good idea." Calhoun smiled.

"Monte, you can't force the girl to work for you if she doesn't want to," Sam said gently. "Let her go."

"Sam's right, Monte. You can't keep Laurette under lock and key," Jarboe said as he swirled the beer in his glass.

"Nobody asked for your opinion, Ox," Calhoun said with a thick tongue. "You comin' with me?"

"Nope, I ain't havin' any hand in kidnapping a woman."

"To hell with both of you, then. I'll do it myself," Calhoun said arrogantly, his loud, drunken voice booming through the nearly empty saloon. He finished his drink, slammed the tumbler down on the polished counter top and turned to leave. "Dammit!" he shouted as he bumped into the stool he'd moved out of the way earlier.

"Wait a minute, Monte." Jarboe grabbed Calhoun's arm, pulled him back. He didn't want Monte making a fool of himself over at the hotel.

"Leave me alone!" Calhoun roared. He jerked his arm free and bounced against the bar in his drunkenness.

"Listen, Monte, there's a better way to fight this thing than kidnapping Laurette."

"Yeah, how?"

Ox Jarboe thought fast. "Hire another singer. There's lots of pretty girls around."

"Not as purty as Laurette," Calhoun whined. He leaned against the bar for support.

"That don't matter, Monte. You put a sexy gal up on that stage and the fellers'll be happy. If she can't sing, maybe she can dance around and wiggle her ass at the customers."

"Yeah," Calhoun said with a lewd smile, his head bobbing as he tried to focus on Jarboe. "A sexy gal. She could dance around the stage without any clothes on. You got good ideas, Ox."

"Not naked, but maybe she could strip out of her clothes while she danced," Jarboe said, his voice full of enthusiasm as he began to believe his own scheme. "That'd get the fellers' juices flowing. You'll pack this place every night."

"Yeah," Calhoun agreed. "After them boys see our little stripper, they won't want to ride out to Bolt's place."

"That's right, Monte."

"Tell you what, Ox. You find me a purty little gal to prance around and take her clothes off up there on that stage," Calhoun slurred, his arm wavering as he pointed to the stage, "and I'll give you part of the action, my good friend." He let his arm fall on Jarboe's shoulder.

"I'll do it, Monte."

"Right away, Ox," Calhoun said. His arm slid off Jarboe's shoulder and he lurched back against the bar.

"It might take me a little time to find the right gal, so I ain't promisin' I can deliver by tonight. But I'll have one here by tomorrow night, for sure."

"Good. Is tomorrow Friday?"

"Yep. And Bolt's gonna be expectin' a big crowd," Jarboe laughed. "Wished to hell I could see his face when they don't show."

"We're gonna be rich," Calhoun said, his words slurred. He waved his arms wildly and staggered back against the bar. "To hell with that bitch Laurette," he shouted. "Give me another drink, Sam. Give everybody a drink."

CHAPTER TEN

"That's the ranch house where Tom and I live." Bolt pointed it out to his three passengers as the horse and buggy pulled onto his property, the spread that he called the Rocking Bar Ranch. All four of them rode squeezed together on the hard driver's seat, which was padded with a thick blanket. Laurette Armand's few possessions rode in the back of the wagon, along with the big wooden trunk that belonged to Ken Selves, and the two carpetbags that held Cherie Bonwit's personal belongings.

"That's a big house," said Laurette, who sat beside him on the crowded seat. "Are you married?"

"No." Bolt laughed, surprised by her question. "Tom and I are bachelors."

"Who does your housework?"

"A woman named Harmony Sanchez usually does our cooking and cleaning, but she left this morning to visit her sick aunt."

"What'll you do while she's gone?"

"Tom and I can fend for ourselves, although the

girls who work for me said they'd help out in Harmony's absence. Guess they don't think we're too swift."

"Does Miss Sanchez live in the house with you?" Laurette asked without batting an eye.

"You're certainly full of questions, young lady." Bolt looked over at Laurette, a playful smile on his lips.

"I didn't mean to pry into your affairs," Laurette said. "I was just curious."

"No, Harmony doesn't live in the ranch house. She lives in the bordello with the girls. She's like a mother to them. She helps them with the chores during the day and then runs the bordello at night to make sure that the girls are treated right."

Laurette's eyebrows shot up. "She's a . . . a madam, then?"

"At night, she is," Bolt said, suddenly irritated by Laurette's questioning and her insinuations.

"It sounds like Miss Sanchez works all day and all night," Laurette commented.

"She does."

Laurette didn't say any more, but Bolt noticed the serious, pensive look on her face.

Tom was out by the stable when the buggy rattled down the sloped path beyond the ranch house. As the buggy bounced along the dirt trail, Laurette and her two companions glanced around, observing the land that spread out in front of them.

Straight ahead of them was the vast expanse of the green, plush lawn that separated the ranch outbuildings from the rustic building of the bordello. On the far side of the expansive yard was a big, neat square of garden space where two of the harlots were working the land with long-handled tools. Dressed in simple gingham frocks and sunbonnets, the two girls looked up and waved when they saw the familiar horse and buggy.

"And that's the bordello where the women who work for me live," Bolt said as he gestured toward the big, two-story log home off to the right of the grass-covered flat land.

"It looks like just an ordinary farm house to me," Laurette said.

"It is." Bolt laughed. "From here you can't see the small cottages out in back of the house where you two ladies will be staying."

Laurette, Cherie and Ken strained their necks as if looking for the cottages.

"That's the stable and the corral over there where Tom is," Bolt said as he pointed off to the left of the green yard. All three passengers turned their heads to look. "That long, flat building beyond the stable is the bunkhouse where my two cowhands live. That's where you'll be staying, Ken."

Selves nodded.

"And that other big building over there is the old barn. We keep the buggy and the spring wagon in there when they're not being used. Keeps them out of the weather."

"And where are all your cattle?" Laurette asked.

Bolt wasn't certain that she was being sarcastic, but it sure as hell sounded like it. Again, he felt the pangs of irritation. "They're out in the pasture. If you look real hard through those trees beyond the garden, you'll likely see some of them."

"I don't see any cattle," Laurette said after several minutes of hard looking.

"They're out there, but I suppose that most of them would be watering down at the river this time of day. If you're so interested in cattle, I'll take you riding out across the pasture in a day or two."

"On a horse?" Laurette asked.

"Of course, on a horse, unless you want to walk."

"I've never been on a horse before."

"We've got some gentle ones." Bolt laughed. "I think you could handle old Bessie."

"What river?" Ken Selves asked. He had been looking in all directions.

"You see those rows of cottonwoods?" Bolt asked, pointing beyond the bunkhouse and the barn.

"Yes," Ken said.

"The river's just below those banks where the trees are growing. You can hear the water running when it's quiet out here, and if you want to walk down to the river sometime, it's not a far piece to walk."

Bolt gestured for Tom to walk over and meet them at the bordello. He tugged the reins to the right and within a couple of minutes, he pulled the buggy up in front of the big log house. He hopped down from the driver's seat and offered his hand to Laurette. On the other side, Ken climbed down and helped Cherie down. By the time Bolt and his three passengers were on the ground, Tom was already halfway across the grassy yard and the two harlots had left the garden and were also walking toward the bordello, their long skirts hiked up in front so they wouldn't trip over them.

"You have lady gardeners?" Laurette asked. She

brushed the trail dust from the folds of her long, full skirt as she watched the two girls who were coming toward them.

Bolt laughed again. "No. Those gals are two of the harlots who work for me."

"Really?" Laurette said. "They don't look like prostitutes."

"What do prostitutes look like?"

"I don't know. I've never seen one. I just thought they'd look like hussies, wenches. You know, a lot of makeup and tight, shameless clothing."

"Only when they're working," Bolt said. "They're decent girls. I think you'll like them."

"And you make them tend to your garden?"

"We've got to eat," Bolt said lightheartedly, trying to ease the tension he sensed in the air.

Cherie Bonwit, who didn't speak or understand much English, seemed lost in the conversation. She smiled anyway.

"How odd," Ken Selves said. "The only gardeners I've seen in New Orleans, and in the East, have been men."

"I can tell you folks haven't spent much time on a farm," Bolt said.

"No. I've never been on a farm," Laurette said. "I thought this was a cattle ranch."

"Same difference as far as the work goes," Bolt said. "On a cattle ranch, you raise cattle. On a farm, you raise crops. Women who live on ranches or farms do a lot of the work, including the gardening, the cleaning, the laundry, the sewing, the cooking, the canning, and milking the cows."

Laurette became indignant. "*Monsieur* Bolt, I

have reservations about working for you after seeing your operation here," she said. "I hope your offer to take us back to town is still good."

Bolt looked at her and saw that she wasn't jesting. "Why would you say that? You haven't met the girls yet. You haven't even seen the bordello where you'll be singing or the cottages where you'll live."

"I've seen quite enough," Laurette said haughtily. "I think you run a slave farm here and I don't want any part of it."

"What do you mean a slave farm?"

"You tell me you make your Miss Sanchez clean your house and do chores all day long, and then you make her work until late at night at your house of sin," Laurette said, a challenging look in her eyes. "Now I see your . . . your harlots working in the fields and I know they must also work tonight to pleasure the vile men who come here."

"You don't understand, Laurie," Bolt said.

"I think I do. You promised me that my friends and I would have some time for relaxation but now I see that your people must work long, arduous hours. I have no desire to be a slave to your whims."

"Are you afraid of a little hard work, Miss Armand?" Bolt said, a sharp edge of sarcasm to his words.

"Not at all, *Monsieur* Bolt. I've worked hard all my life. But there is a limit to one's endurance. I'm afraid I couldn't do chores all day long and still give a decent performance at night. Even the Lord rested on the seventh day."

"You'll have plenty of time to rest. You don't have to do anything here but sing, Laurie."

"That's what you say, but I see differently," she said, her nose in the air.

"Give us a chance, will you?" Bolt said. "I think you'll be pleasantly surprised by the cheerful atmosphere around here."

"Hello again, Miss Armand," Tom said as he joined the group.

"You remember Tom Penrod, don't you?" Bolt said to Laurette.

"Yes, of course. Hello, Tom."

Bolt stepped over to Cherie Bonwit. "Cherie, this is Tom," he said. He put his hand on Tom's shoulder to indicate what he meant. "Tom," he repeated.

Cherie nodded. *"Oui. Monsieur* Tom." She smiled shyly at Tom.

Bolt turned to Laurette. "Tell Cherie to just call him Tom."

"Never mind about that, Miss Armand," Tom said with a big grin. "I like the way Cherie says my name just fine."

Bolt tugged Tom's sleeve, pulled him over to the prissy piano player who stood with his hands behind his back. Selves was wearing his gray, broadcloth suit and the derby hat. "Ken, this is Tom Penrod," Bolt said. "I guess you two already know each other."

"Yes, I've seen him before," Selves said as he offered his hand. "Mr. Penrod," he nodded.

Tom took his hand and shook it. "You can call me Tom."

"And these are two of the girls who live here," Bolt said as the two pretty harlots walked up. He introduced Doreen Jenson, a tall, healthy looking girl, and Linda Ramsey, a lovely blonde, to the newcomers. "Laurette will be singing at the bordello starting tomorrow night, and Ken Selves is her talented pianist," he said.

"Good. Friday night is a good time to start," said Linda. "Welcome to all of you. I hope you'll like it here."

"I hope so, too," Laurette said. "However, I'm not sure we'll be staying long enough to find out."

"You'll like it here," Doreen assured her. "Bolt's a pretty fair boss."

"Thanks, Doreen, I needed that." Bolt smiled. "Will you and Cathy take these two ladies inside and introduce them to the other girls?"

"Sure. We'd be happy to," Doreen said.

"They'll be staying in the two newest cottages out back, so after Laurette and Cherie have seen the house, you can take them to their rooms so they can rest up before supper. Laurie, do you want all of your things unpacked?"

Laurette glanced over at the writing table and the comfortable chair in the back of the wagon. "No, just my two bags for now," she said. "No sense in unpacking the other things until I decide whether or not I'm going to stay."

Bolt unfastened the leather straps that held the luggage in place. He set Laurette's two carpetbags on the ground, then reached back to get Cherie's two smaller bags.

Tom stepped forward and picked up the two heaviest pieces of luggage. "I'll escort the ladies to their cottages," he said.

"I figured you would, Tom," Bolt said. "I'll take

Ken on over to the bunkhouse and help him unload his trunk. Are Chet and Rusty over there?"

"Yeah, they came in from the pasture a little while ago."

"Bolt, we're planning on you and Tom eating with us tonight," Doreen said. "We're cooking a big pot roast for supper, so there's plenty for everyone."

"Sounds good."

"We'll eat at six o'clock, so don't be late."

"We'll be here," Bolt said as he and Ken climbed back up in the driver's seat of the buggy.

Doreen reached down and picked up the two lighter bags. "Come on, ladies," she said to Laurette and Cherie. "We'll show you around and then you'll have a couple of hours to rest before supper's ready."

Bolt noticed the apprehensive look on Laurette's face as she followed Doreen up the steps to the bordello. He halfway expected her to turn around and climb back in the buggy before she got to the door.

After supper, Doreen and Cathy Boring, a feisty red-haired harlot, got up from the large dining room table and started to clear the dirty dishes away.

Ken Selves rose, too. "If you people will excuse me, I want to go over to the bunkhouse and get settled in. Thank you for supper. It was very good."

"Thank you," said Winny Hart, a dark-haired beauty who had done most of the cooking.

Selves walked around the table and stood near Bolt. "Your cowhands, Chet and Rusty, have made me quite comfortable over at the bunkhouse. They said for me to tell you that they would put up the partition to make a separate room for me."

"Good. I figured they'd do it," Bolt said. "And, Ken, you don't have to wear a suit and tie at meals around here."

Ken looked down at his broadcloth suit. "I have only suits," he said.

"We'll see that you get some clothes more suited to ranch life," Bolt said.

"Thank you. Good night, everyone."

"Ken, will you come back over and play the piano for us in a little while?" Cathy Boring asked.

"I think not," Ken said shyly.

"Oh, please," Cathy begged. "Laurie says you're a concert pianist, and she says you're really good."

"Please, Ken," Doreen chimed in. "We would appreciate it if you'd play for us. We don't get much culture out here."

"I beg your pardon, Doreen," Bolt said. "Don't you think I'm cultured?" He sat up taller, straightened his collar.

"Cultured in what? Shoeing a horse?" Doreen asked.

All the girls laughed, including Laurette.

"There's a fine art to it," Bolt said.

"Please come back and play for us, Ken," Doreen said. "As you can see, we're starved for some refinement around here."

"Yes, please," Cathy pleaded. "Just give us time to clear up the dishes and get dressed for the evening. We'll be forever grateful."

"But you will be busy with . . . with the . . . the other men by then," Ken said.

"Not until much later tonight, probably," Doreen said. "It would be such fun to sit in the parlor and watch you play."

"Only if you lovely ladies will sing the songs I play." Ken smiled timidly and Bolt realized that it was the first time he'd ever seen the man smile.

"There isn't a one of us who can carry a tune," Cathy laughed, "except Laurie, of course."

"I can play the piano for Miss Armand anytime," Ken said in his thin, squeaky voice. "For you ladies, I will play only if you will sing along with me."

"You've got a deal," Cathy said. "Come back in an hour and we'll be ready."

Selves glanced at each of the girls. "What a lovely choir you will make." With that, he turned on his heel and marched out of the room.

Bolt swore there was a lighter air about Ken's step as he walked across the room. He turned to Laurette, who was sitting on his right at the crowded dining room table. "Ken's quite a rascal, isn't he?"

"It appears he is." Laurette smiled. "That's a side of Ken I've never seen before. He's always been so shy with the ladies. Somehow, I just can't picture him in the middle of six beautiful girls. Especially women of the night."

"Neither can I." Bolt laughed. "And speaking of beautiful women, Laurie, would you like to go out on the front porch and watch the sun set?" he asked as he scooted his chair back and stood up.

Laurette set her linen napkin on the table, pushed her chair back and stood up. "I should help the girls with the dishes," she said.

"Not tonight, Laurie." Doreen smiled. "Go on

and enjoy the evening."

"But, you girls prepared the meal," Laurette said. "I wouldn't feel right if Cherie and I didn't help you clear up the mess."

"You and Cherie are our guests tonight," Doreen said firmly. "Tomorrow, we'll consider you family and then if you want to give us a hand, we'll gladly accept."

A look of surprise came over Laurette's face. "It's been a long time since I've had a family," she said, her voice filled with sadness. She stared down as she pushed her chair in, then looked up and smiled at Doreen. "That sounds fair enough," she said. "Maybe Cherie and I will cook supper tomorrow evening." She glanced over at Cherie. "Yes, Cherie?"

Cherie grinned. *"Oui.* Yes," she said and then shrugged her shoulders, indicating that she didn't understand what she'd consented to.

"She'll agree to anything." Linda Ramsey laughed. She stood and started gathering up the soiled napkins from the table.

All the girls laughed and shouted, *"oui,"* in unison.

Bolt was pleased by the cheerful rapport between Laurette and the six girls who worked for him. He knew his girls were happy with the life they'd chosen for themselves. They had all the freedom they wanted and if one of them didn't feel up to working on a particular night, she knew she could take the night off and still collect a full week's pay. And although they did enjoy going to town on certain occasions, or riding horseback through the countryside, they usually preferred to stay at home. For the most part, they were happy little homemakers who took pride in their surroundings.

Bolt hadn't done much talking during supper and even if he'd wanted to, he wouldn't have had much of a chance to do so. The girls had chattered like magpies all through the meal and Bolt was content to sit back and observe them. He was particularly interested in seeing Laurette's reaction to being around the harlots. She had come to the Rocking Bar Ranch with the attitude that she was above such tainted women who worked as shameless bawdy girls, but he could see that Laurette was quite comfortable with the girls. Even Cherie Bonwit, who couldn't speak much English, seemed to enjoy being around the other girls.

He wondered about it, though. Perhaps Miss Armand would not have been so tolerant of the prostitutes if she had first seen the girls in their heavy makeup and their skimpy harlot costumes.

Tom rose from the table. He had been sitting next to Cherie and across the table from Bolt. He stepped over behind Cherie's chair. "Come, my Cherie. I shall escort you to your castle," he said gallantly.

Cherie turned her head and looked up at him with a shy smile. *"Oui, Monsieur Tom."*

"Oui, oui," Tom said. He pulled out Cherie's chair and when she stood, he bowed and offered her his arm.

The other girls giggled.

Bolt rolled his eyes upward and shook his head at Tom's mockery. "You sound like a damned pig, Tom."

"You ought to know, Bolt. You spend a lot of time

with pigs," Tom said over his shoulder as he escorted Miss Bonwit out of the dining room and toward the back door.

"I didn't know you had pigs," Laurette said to Bolt, a puzzled look on her face.

Again, the harlots laughed.

"We don't," Bolt said. "Tom's trying to be funny, but he's not."

"I don't understand."

"Don't try," Cathy Boring said as she whisked a stack of dirty plates off the table. "Bolt and Tom tease each other unmercifully."

Doreen walked by and picked up some of the dirty utensils. "If you two are going to watch the sun set," she said, "you'd better get going before it's all over with."

"Shall we?" Bolt said. He stuck his arm out.

"It would be my pleasure, *Monsieur* Bolt."

CHAPTER ELEVEN

"It's beautiful, isn't it?" Laurette sighed as she leaned against the porch railing and gazed out at the wide expanse of fiery sky. She was still wearing the same pretty blue dress she'd worn all day, but she hadn't worn the feathery hat since they'd arrived at the ranch late that afternoon. Before supper, she had untied the ribbon that held her hair at the back of her head and brushed out her tight curls. Her long, dark hair now hung softly about her face.

"There's nothing like a western sunset," Bolt said. He rested his arms on the top of the railing and leaned against the weathered boards. Although he looked out at the sky, he was well aware of the closeness of the beautiful woman beside him. The same cool breeze that seemed to blow the heat out of the lingering day, brought Laurette's delicate scent to him on its wavering air currents.

They had come out on the porch in time to see the last glowing tip of the fire ball sink into the horizon and disappear. The puffs of clouds, that had been tinged with bright pink and salmon clouds, were already taking on the darker hues of red and crimson.

"Can you see the sunset from your house?" she asked. She turned to glance at the large, sprawling house on the hill above them.

Bolt turned, too, and looked up at his house. "From the kitchen window, or from the back porch," he said, "and then, almost every morning, I watch the sunrise from my living room while I'm finishing my coffee."

"I'm rarely up early enough to see the break of dawn," she admitted as she turned back to watch the clouds that were slowly turning purple.

"Then you're missing the best part of the day," Bolt said. "I seldom miss a sunrise or a sunset."

"You surprise me, Bolt."

"Why?"

"I didn't think men cared about such things."

"We've got feelings, too." Bolt smiled. "Anyone who doesn't stop long enough to enjoy nature's beauty once in a while has got a heart of stone."

"Why, you sentimental old fool," Laurette said affectionately. "I didn't know you had it in you."

"There are a lot of things you don't know about me." Bolt laughed.

He sensed that she was staring at him and, as he turned his head back to the west, he looked over at her, once again stunned by her haunting beauty, her searching blue eyes, her sensual lips. They gazed into each other's eyes for what seemed like a long, awkward time to Bolt and yet, he couldn't look away from her. He wondered what she was thinking.

Could she tell that he was smitten with her? Did she know how very much he wanted to be with her? Did she feel anything at all for him?

Laurette finally spoke. "Maybe you'll invite me up to your house for a cup of coffee some early morning and we can watch the sunrise together."

Bolt swallowed hard, surprised by the boldness he saw in her expressive eyes, her blue eyes that now sparkled with the dark purple of the sky. And was there a husk in her voice? Or had he just imagined it? Either way, her casual remark had sounded like a bold proposition.

"You're welcome at my house anytime, Laurie," Bolt said, leaving the invitation open to her, hoping she didn't notice the husk in his own voice.

"I just may do that one of these mornings," she said, not committing herself.

"You're staying, then?" he asked.

She gave him a smile that was part coyness, part smugness. "For now," she said.

"Good. I'm glad to hear it."

"I was wrong about your girls, Bolt," she said, turning serious. "They're really nice. All of them. They've been very kind to both Cherie and me."

"I tried to tell you they were nice girls."

"I know," Laurette said with a sheepish grin, "but before I met the girls, I had them pictured in my mind as wanton hussies, as brazen prostitutes who wore skimpy, vulgar outfits and painted their lips bright red."

"They are brazen prostitutes," Bolt said. "At least at night they are."

"I know. I find it hard to believe."

"Will you change your mind about them being nice girls when you see them all gussied up in their skimpy outfits and their bright red lipstick? Will you think less of them when you see them brazenly teasing the men who come here? That's what they do, you know."

"That's hard to answer, Bolt." Laurette was quiet for a moment. "No, I won't think less of them. I know those girls are good and decent, and caring. Besides, it's not my place to judge others."

"But you did," Bolt said, "before you met them."

"Yes, because I didn't understand." Laurette sighed. "I still don't understand how such nice, decent girls could become prostitutes. Why do they do it, Bolt?"

"I don't know. You'll have to ask them." He glanced up at the sky. The clouds were gray now and, like the pale, darkening sky, the grass and the trees had given up their color for the day. It was the time of evening, just before darkness closed in, when everything across the land was bathed in a final, colorless glow.

"I will," Laurette said as she gazed out at the shadowy landscape. Suddenly startled, she jumped and grabbed Bolt's arm, squeezed it. "What was that?" she cried.

"What is it, Laurie?" Bolt put his hand on hers and followed her gaze.

"That noise." Laurette turned her head to listen. "There it is again." She tightened her grip on Bolt's arm.

Bolt heard it then. He smiled and patted her hand. "That was a cow, Laurie. I'm so used to hearing them, I didn't even notice."

Laurette took her hand away from his arm and patted her chest as she let out a big sigh. "You really do have cattle then, don't you?"

"Yep. That's the only thing I know that moos like that."

"I guess I should have gone with my first impression of you." Laurette laughed.

"And what was that?" Bolt raised his eyebrows.

"When I first saw you that night at the Prairie Schooner, you defended my honor and I thought you were a kind, honest man. Handsome, too," she added with a teasing flash of her eyes.

"And you changed your mind about all those things after you got to know me," he said.

"For a while I did. Oh, I still thought you were handsome," she said with a little shrug of her shoulders, "but when I heard you talking about how hard Harmony Sanchez worked, and then I saw Doreen and Linda toiling in the garden, I decided that you were a slave driver. I figured you sat up there in your fancy house and counted your money while the others did all the work for you."

"Doesn't sound like a bad idea," Bolt said.

"The girls told me different. They said you and Tom worked harder than anyone else around here."

"We all work hard."

"The girls also told me that you don't charge them room and board. They consider the Rocking Bar Ranch their home."

"I gave them a place to live and a place to work. They earn their keep."

"You're a generous man, *Monsieur* Bolt."

"And you are a very beautiful woman, Miss Armand." He smiled.

A stiff breeze whirled around them and riffled through Laurette's hair. She shivered and snuggled her arm against Bolt's. He slid his arm around her shoulder and drew her close.

It was fully dark now, except for the golden rays of lamplight that spilled from the parlor windows and splashed across the porch. Even though the curtains were closed, Bolt was glad that he and Laurette were at the far end of the porch where the light didn't touch them.

"Are you cold?" he asked.

"Not really. Just confused." She turned to face him.

"About what?" Bolt turned sideways and put a hand on each of her shoulders. He caught a whiff of her heady perfume and wanted more than anything to take her in his arms and never let her go.

"I don't know." Laurette took a deep breath and let it out slowly. "It's so peaceful out here, and I feel so good about being here. . . ."

"Then what's the problem?"

"I still have reservations about singing in a bordello. It seems wrong to me. I have the eerie feeling that once it turns dark, like it is now, that everything is going to turn evil and ugly."

"And the vampires are going to come out?" Bolt teased.

"I'm serious, Bolt," she said. "I had the same fears as a child and now they're all coming back to me. As a little girl, I always dreaded the coming of night and darkness and, right now, I've got that same scared feeling. It's like I know I'm going to have a bad dream and, if I can keep it from turning dark, everything will be all right."

"A lot of people are afraid of the dark, Laurie," Bolt said as he squeezed her shoulders.

"It's more than that, Bolt. Being here, I know that everything is going to change at night. That house is going to change into a house of sin. The parlor will become a place of orgy. The girls will turn into wanton witches. It will all be unreal to me and I don't think I can handle it."

"I don't think you'll find it as repulsive as you've got it pictured in your mind, Laurette. The parlor is a meeting place and there won't be any orgies in there. Except for the revealing costumes the girls wear and the mild flirtations that go on in the parlor, I don't think you'll find anything offensive. After all, those gals are just as private as you are and whatever they do with the customers is done behind closed doors."

"The way you say it doesn't make it sound so bad," Laurette sighed, "but I still don't know."

"Give it time, Laurie," he said. "If you find you don't like it here, you're free to leave."

Laurie took a deep breath and shook the bad thoughts from her mind.

"You're a decent chap, Bolt. I like you." She tipped her head up, parted her lips as if she were inviting him to kiss her.

"I like you, too."

Bolt couldn't resist the temptation. He lowered his head and brushed his lips against hers. He was surprised that she didn't resist him. Again, he placed his mouth gently on hers and found her lips wet and supple as she responded to his kiss.

Hungry for affection, Laurette snuggled close to him, slid her arms around his waist and thrust her body against his. When he felt the tip of her hot tongue slip into his mouth, a warm glow flooded through his loins. He wrapped his arms around her, drew her even closer and the kiss lasted a long time.

Laurette finally broke the kiss and pulled away from him. "We'd better go in now," she said.

Bolt noticed the quivering husk in her voice and knew that she'd been as affected by their passionate kiss as he had.

"Yeah, we'd better," he sighed.

"It's been a tiring day," she said as they started toward the front door. "I think I'll go inside and say good night to everyone and then go on back to my cottage and retire early."

"Do you want me to walk you to your cottage?" he asked.

As Laurette passed in front of the window, the soft lamplight struck her face with a radiant glow. She looked over at him and smiled.

"Just to my door, Bolt," she said. "I don't trust myself to be alone with you right now."

Bolt didn't see Laurette again until supper time the following night, Friday evening, and even then, he didn't have much of a chance to talk to her. She and Cherie had helped prepare the meal and as soon as everyone was done eating, the two French girls had jumped up to help with the dishes.

Bolt had spent the morning in town. While Laurette and the others were packing their bags the day before, he had ordered flyers announcing Laurette's appearance at the Rocking Bar. He had paid the printer an extra five dollars to tack them up around town and he wanted to make sure it was done. He also wanted to hire a band for Laurette's opening night. He had discussed it with Ken Selves the night before and Ken had agreed that having a small band would make the evening special for Laurette.

The flyers were posted all over town by the time he got there, so he rode straight to the Bluebelle Supper Club where he managed to hire four musicians from the Bluebelle orchestra for the night—a violinist, two fiddlers, and the drummer. The band wouldn't be very big, but with Ken Selves at the piano, it would be enough. While he was there, he also hired two bartenders to handle the crowd that he expected at the bordello that night.

After buying the bread and cheese he wanted for the party, and enough blue velvet material to make a curtain for the stage, Bolt had ridden on home.

He and Tom had spent all afternoon getting the stage ready. They had hung the velvet drapes and extended the curtain far enough to one side so that Laurette could enter the stage from the hallway without being seen until the curtain opened. They had nailed together some steps at that end of the stage and then placed candles at the front edge of the platform to serve as footlights. Tom had brought in a ladder and set it to one side of the stage. Chet, the young red-headed cowhand who worked for Bolt, had agreed to stand on the ladder during Laurette's performance and hold a lantern high enough to light her face.

Now, with supper over and the stage set except for the flowers he'd asked Doreen to bring in from the yard, Bolt knew that there would be a lull before the customers started arriving.

Knowing that the girls would be busy changing into their fancy, bawdy outfits after they finished the dishes and not wanting to sit and listen to the small orchestra practicing Laurette's songs with Ken Selves when the musicians arrived shortly, Bolt wandered up the hill to the ranch house to put on a clean shirt. Tom, who had shaved and changed shirts before supper, chose to stay down at the bordello.

Bolt was nervous, fidgety, as he walked up the steps to the ranch house. He knew Laurette would be, too, and he wondered if he wasn't suffering for her.

He knew one thing for sure. He didn't want anything to go wrong tonight. He didn't want to risk losing Laurette.

CHAPTER TWELVE

Bolt didn't walk back down to the bordello until seven thirty, a half an hour before they would open for business. Laurette wouldn't come on stage until another half hour after that. He wanted everyone settled down before he brought her out.

Tom and the musicians were the only ones in the large parlor when he walked in. The music was loud, off key, but Ken was working with the other musicians to bring the tune into harmony. The scent of perfume already filled the room, even though the harlots were still upstairs.

He thought about walking over to Laurette's cottage to see how she was faring, but decided against it. He was sure that Laurette would be very nervous and he didn't want to add to it. Besides, she was probably busy getting dressed for her performance and most likely, Cherie Bonwit was there helping her.

"It looks nice in here," Bolt said as he glanced around the huge, tidy room.

Tom got up from the sofa and strolled over to Bolt. "Doreen brought the flowers in a few minutes ago." He nodded toward the stage.

"Oh, good, she remembered." Bolt glanced over at the stage and saw the crystal vase that sat on Ken's piano below the stage. The vase was filled with a beautiful arrangement of freshly cut flowers. Two bigger, flower-filled vases sat on the stage in front of the musicians, positioned so that Laurette would stand between them when she sang. If Monte Calhoun couldn't provide her with flowers for her opening night, he would, he thought.

"Laurette should like them," he said. "I hope we have a good crowd."

"Bolt, are you going to need me here tonight?" Tom asked.

Bolt frowned and looked at Tom suspiciously. "Why? You got other plans?"

"Not right away. I'll stick around here until things get rolling and then I thought I'd go over to Cherie's cottage for awhile."

"Oh?"

"She's gonna teach me to speak French," Tom said with a sheepish grin.

"I'll bet. You know damned well why you're going over there and so do I."

"Don't get testy with me, Bolt. Just 'cause Laurette turned you down, no need to take it out on me." Tom smiled smugly.

"How could she turn me down? I didn't even ask her," Bolt retorted.

"Maybe not, but you wanted to," Tom joked.

"Hell, you were droolin' all over yourself when you took her out to watch the sunset last night. Nice romantic setting like that. I knew what you had in mind. You didn't fool anybody."

"I wasn't trying to fool anybody. We watched the sunset. That's all."

"Oh? Too bad she didn't tumble."

"Go ahead and go to your damned French lesson," Bolt snarled, even though he did it in jest. "I sure as hell don't need a smart-ass like you around."

"Thanks, Bolt. I had a feeling that's what you'd say."

"And don't wear yourself out. I want you checking back in here every half hour or so if we've got a big crowd in here tonight."

"That ain't fair, Bolt. What can I accomplish in half-hour intervals?"

"You're like a rabbit, Tom. You can accomplish everything you're got planned in two minutes flat." Bolt laughed.

"Not true. I'll need at least an hour or two without interruption. French isn't an easy language to learn, you know."

"You don't need to learn much, Tom. I'm sure you can make Cherie understand what you want without uttering a word."

"I'm sure I can," Tom boasted, "but I don't want to be rushed."

"Sorry to spoil your plans, but I need you here."

"But why do you need me?" Tom sulked. "Chet and Rusty will be over here to help you, and the bartenders will be here. Hell, Rusty's big enough to handle five men at once."

"Because I don't want trouble here tonight," Bolt said.

"How about every hour instead of every half hour?" Tom asked.

"I may not need you at all," Bolt said, "but stick around long enough for us to size up the crowd."

"I planned to do that anyway."

"This is an important night for all of us. Laurette is nervous enough about singing in a bordello and if there's any trouble at all, she'll quit. And if she quits, Cherie goes with her."

"I see what you mean."

Bolt looked over at the front door when he heard it open. Jimmy Willaker, one of the regulars at the Rocking Bar Bordello, walked in with a big smile on his face. Jimmy was a little slow-witted, and boring at times, but he never caused any trouble.

"Howdy," Willaker said as he ambled across the room. "Sure smells good in here."

"You're a little early, Jimmy," Bolt said.

"I know," said Willaker. His proud smile was like that of a simpleton. "I come over early so's I could get me a place where I can see that purty singer up close. Where is she?" He peered at the stage where the musicians were rehearsing.

"She'll be here in a little while," Bolt said. "Don't worry, Jimmy, you'll be first in line. You can pick any place in the room."

"Good. I wasn't lucky enough to get one of them tables up front like you fellers did that first night Laurette sung at the Prairie Schooner."

"Yeah, Tom and I were pretty lucky that night,"

Bolt said.

"Hell, I went back to see her every damned night she was there, but I never could scrape enough money together to buy me a seat at one of them tables near the stage."

"Well, you'll see her tonight, Jimmy. You want a drink?" Not wanting to get involved in one of Willaker's long, boring stories just then, Bolt strolled over and walked around behind the bar to check the glasses and the liquor supply, even though he'd already done it.

The music stopped abruptly and started again after Ken had spoken to the drummer. This time the melody was played softer and more in tune.

"Maybe just a beer," Jimmy said as he followed Bolt to the bar. "I sure don't want to get drunk tonight. I want to keep my head clear so's I can see Laurette real good." Awkward in his movements, he climbed onto one of the high bar stools.

"You want a drink, Tom?" Bolt asked as he turned to the wooden keg behind him and filled a tumbler with beer. Foam spilled over the brim of the glass as he slid it across the counter to Jimmy.

"Yeah, I'll have a whiskey," Tom said. He ambled over and eased onto a bar stool at the end of the counter, closest to the stage.

Bolt wiped up the spilled beer with a bar towel, then set two smaller tumblers on the counter. He poured them half full of whiskey, slid one across to Tom and kept the other for himself.

"You might not get much of a crowd here tonight," Jimmy said after he took a swallow of the beer.

"You don't think so?" Bolt said, wondering why Jimmy had made such a remark.

"Not if Monte Calhoun can get the fellers comin' into the Schooner to see that new gal he's got." Jimmy shook his head sadly, as if he were delivering news of a kin's death.

"Oh? Calhoun's got another singer?" Tom asked.

"Not a singer. A stripper," Jimmy said.

"A stripper?" Bolt said.

"I thought you knew," Jimmy said. "Hell, Calhoun's got posters up all over town."

"I sure as hell didn't see them when I was in there this morning," Bolt said. He took a sip of his whiskey and thought about what this would do to his party for Laurette's opening night.

"Well, they're there, Bolt. Every place you got a poster up, Calhoun's got one up." Jimmy wiggled around on the bar stool and sat up taller. He grinned as if he were suddenly important because he knew more than they did. "And most of 'em are tacked up right on top of your flyers, so's yours don't show."

"That bastard," Bolt mumbled.

"Calhoun's posters ain't fancy like they was before," Jimmy said with wide-eyed enthusiasm, as if he were trying to ease Bolt's grief. "No pictures or nothin' on 'em."

"Then maybe nobody will pay any attention to them," Tom said.

"Probably not." Jimmy grinned. "Hell, they're just big squares of paper with the words "SEE ALL OF LOLA AT THE PRAIRIE SCHOONER" scribbled on 'em in pencil. Nothin' to worry about." He shook his head.

"No. I guess not." Bolt turned his head away and

watched the musicians. He sensed that Jimmy was prepared to tell a long, dull tale and he wasn't in the mood to listen.

"Of course the word "ALL" is underlined and that's what caused all the commotion over the big banner," Jimmy added, as if it were an afterthought.

"What commotion?" Tom said.

"What banner?" Bolt asked. His head spun around and he faced Jimmy again.

Jimmy Willaker smiled. "Calhoun strung himself up a big, high banner in town. It stretches all the way across the street. I was right there and watched him and his men string it up. Right in the middle of town. Hard to miss." He made himself comfortable on the stool, prepared to tell his story. "Seems them Christian women got wind of it. You know, them do-gooders who's always tryin' to tell you what's decent and what ain't. The Christian Women's Society."

"Yeah. Go on," Bolt said impatiently.

"Well, them old biddies come a'runnin' from every direction when they heard about that banner bein' strung up across the street. They was like a bunch of hens with their feathers ruffled. I mean they kicked up their heels." Jimmy stopped to laugh. "Them women was fixin' to tear down that banner, but somebody stopped 'em. They could'a done it, too. That banner was just made of butcher paper, ya know. I forgot to tell you that Calhoun had went back to his saloon by that time. But anyways, when those old hens started to rip down that banner, one of Calhoun's men spoke up for him. That's when all the commotion started."

"Get on with it, Jimmy," Bolt said. "Did they tear the banner down or not?"

"I'm gettin' to it." Jimmy grinned proudly. "Them women was claimin' that the banner was sinful. Not the banner. Just the words written on it was sinful."

Bolt sighed with frustration. He glanced at Tom, rolled his eyes up and shook his head.

Tom smiled, shrugged his shoulders.

"Anyways, that's when all the arguin' began," Jimmy continued, oblivious to the fact that Bolt and Tom were bored with his story. "Funniest thing I ever saw. Them frumpy old Christian women was sayin' that the message on the banner was sinful in the eyes of the Lord, and that they was gonna tear it down and burn it up. Of course, Calhoun's men insisted that them women had better leave it be if they didn't want to get their big, fat noses chopped off for stickin' them in where they didn't belong."

Jimmy Willaker laughed at that. He paused long enough to take a drink of beer. "Purty soon, a whole bunch of people started gathering right under that there banner," he said, shifting positions on the stool. "Why, I'll bet most of the people of San Antonio showed up before it was all over with. And everybody was shouting at everybody else. You never heard such cursin' in your life."

Willaker shook his head and then continued. "Them Christian women was shoutin' right back, too, with their cries of hellfire and damnation. All that screamin' nearly busted my ears. You should'a heard it. Of course, most of the businessmen was sidin' with them high and mighty, righteous old gals, but a lot of them fellers was stickin' up for Calhoun, too. You never saw such a crowd gathered in that street before. A block each way, at least. You'da thought they'd come to see a hangin'."

"So, did the banner come down or is it still up there?" Tom asked, not really caring by now.

"I was just gettin' to that there part," Jimmy said. "After all that shoutin' and hollerin', and the pushin' and shovin' that went on in the street, that big feller, Ox Jarboe, he just stepped right up there and took charge of things. He looked mean as hell. I wouldn't want to meet up with Ox on a dark street. You know who Ox Jarboe is, don't ya?"

Jimmy looked at Bolt, but didn't wait for his answer. "Ox Jarboe's a friend of Monte Calhoun's," he went on. "A great big bull of a feller. Hair growin' all over his face and his beard goes halfway down to his belly button." Jimmy made the appropriate gestures as he spoke, spreading his arms wide above his head to indicate how big Jarboe was, then rubbing his cheeks, and finally putting one open hand, palm up, across his chest, as if to measure Jarboe's beard. "Looks like he just come down outta some mountain."

"Yes, we know who Ox Jarboe is." Bolt sighed.

"Yeah, of course you do." Jimmy nodded. "You probably seen him in at the Prairie Schooner. He sits in there most days. Most nights, too, now that I think about it. Always got a beer in front of him. Well, anyways, Ox just climbs up on that there ladder . . . it was the very same ladder they had used to string up the banner."

"Naturally," Tom said. He looked at Bolt, shook his head.

"Yeah," Jimmy went on, as if Tom hadn't spoken, "and Ox climbs up there and tries to get everybody's attention. Which, of course, he can't because of all the yellin' and screamin' that's goin' on down below him and hardly nobody sees him goin' up there in the first place anyway."

"Jeeez!" Tom exploded. "I ain't following you at all." He shook his head, clamped his hands on his head as if he couldn't believe what he was hearing.

"Sorry, Tom. All right now, I'll tell that part over again. Ox Jarboe climbs up on this ladder, see," Jimmy said, speaking very slowly and distinctly.

"Never mind," Bolt said, "Just go on with it, Jimmy. We don't have much time."

"I know. Well, anyways, here's this Ox Jarboe up on that ladder and nobody payin' him no mind, so he draws out his pistol and fires a shot in the air. Well, let me tell you, that got everybody's attention real quick. Scared the socks offa me and I knew he was gonna shoot that damned thing 'cause I was watchin' him all the time. Only I thought he was gonna start shootin' them damned, pesky women."

"So everybody's looking up at Jarboe . . ." Bolt said, trying to hurry the story along.

"They sure was," Jimmy nodded. "Everybody in that street was lookin' up there at Jarboe. That's when Ox Jarboe made his challenge to them church women."

"What challenge?" Bolt asked, knowing that if he didn't ask that question, Jimmy would go around the mulberry bush before he got to the point.

"Well, since them church ladies was claimin' that the banner was sinful, Ox told 'em that if they could point out any one word on the banner that was sinful, or vulgar, or even offensive to anyone in the crowd, that he would personally tear the banner down. Now that's a fair offer, don't you think?"

Bolt didn't answer.

Jimmy Willaker took another sip of his beer and it seemed to Bolt that Jimmy was trying to think if he'd forgotten any of the details.

"Well, of course, them women was stumped on that one," Jimmy said after a minute. "They couldn't find a single word that was sinful or vulgar. Of course, they tried their best to claim that the line under the word "ALL" was the thing that made the banner sinful because they said the line meant that Lola was gonna be takin' all of her clothes off. Which is what I thought, too. Wouldn't you think that's what it meant?"

"Yeah," Bolt mumbled.

"Well, when them uppity women kept insisting that that damned line was sinful, of course they just got laughed at. Ox Jarboe even called down to some of them men who had sided with them church women and asked 'em if that word "ALL" was sinful, and none of 'em said it was. And then Jarboe asks if the line itself was sinful and, of course, them men laughed again and said the line weren't sinful."

"So the banner stayed up?" Bolt said.

"For the time being," Jimmy said. "Them church women was madder'n hell, so they told Jarboe that they was gonna call a town meeting in the morning ... that's tomorrow morning ... and that they guaranteed Ox Jarboe that the banner would be torn down before noon."

"Well, Calhoun got what he wanted out of it, didn't he?" Tom said. He took a drink of whiskey and set the glass back on the counter.

"You mean all that attention because of the banner?" Jimmy asked. "Yeah, that was what I was thinkin', too."

"Yeah," said Bolt. "It won't matter if they take the banner down tomorrow. That bastard has already gotten all that free advertising for the Prairie Schooner with that little stunt."

"Not a person in town don't know about it," Jimmy agreed. "But don't worry about it, though. I don't think he'll have many customers tonight, not even with Lola there."

"A stripper should bring in a big crowd," Tom said. "That is, if the church ladies don't shut it down first."

"Well, a lot of the fellers I talked to said they wasn't goin' to the Prairie Schooner anyway. Not even with Lola there."

"Why not?" Bolt said. He glanced over at the door and saw three more customers come in. The two bartenders he had hired came in right behind the three men. The musicians stopped practicing and, after closing the velvet curtains on the stage so that it would be ready for Laurette's entrance, they walked on outside for some air.

"They said Calhoun has pulled the wool over their eyes too damned many times before," Jimmy said, "and they ain't gonna waste no more money havin' it done to 'em again."

"Maybe they're finally getting wise to his tricks," Bolt said.

"Yeah," said Jimmy. "Besides, them fellers wanta see Laurette. You'll have a good crowd tonight."

Bolt was beginning to think that Jimmy Willaker was right as the room began filling up with customers who were as anxious to see Laurette Armand sing as they were to take one of the pretty soiled doves to bed.

The six harlots came down the staircase a few minutes later and they all looked stunning and seductive in their tight, skimpy outfits that revealed a lot of bare flesh.

When the harlots began mingling with the randy men, teasing them with their sexual charms, the huge room began to look and feel more like a bordello than a simple parlor.

And that's what worried Bolt. How would Laurette react to the change in the room? Laurette had continually expressed her nervousness about singing in a house of prostitution and, even though she knew about the bordello, would she find it too repulsive for her tastes? Would she walk out and never come back?

"When is Laurette Armand gonna be here?" Jimmy Willaker asked as he stared at the closed curtain on the stage.

"In about a half an hour," Bolt said.

"That long?" Jimmy said. The disappointment showed all over his face. "It's already eight o'clock."

"We'll give the fellows a chance to get a drink if they want it and, as soon as they settle down, we'll bring Laurette out."

"I think I'll go on up and stand by the stage so's I can get a good look at her when the curtain opens,"

Jimmy said as he eased down from the bar stool.

"Good idea, Jimmy," Bolt said.

"Did I tell you how I tried to sneak up to one of them front tables at the Prairie Schooner one night so's I could see Laurette up close?" Jimmy asked.

"No, you'll have to tell me about it sometime," Bolt said, "but right now you'd better get a place to stand before someone else takes your spot."

"You're right." Jimmy took his half-full glass of beer and went to stand right in front of the stage.

Bolt glanced at the throng of men who were streaming through the front door. He was glad for the business. He just prayed that nothing would go wrong that night.

CHAPTER THIRTEEN

In the town of San Antonio, two miles away from Bolt's Rocking Bar Bordello, Monte Calhoun's luck had turned sour.

Lola, his new star attraction, had just stepped out onto the stage and there weren't more than two dozen customers in the saloon. And the men who were there were drunk and rowdy.

Lola wore a red silk kimono that looked like an old, faded bathrobe. And Calhoun wasn't impressed with the girl's looks, either. Although Ox Jarboe had assured him that Lola was young, pretty, and full-breasted, she looked short and chubby, too old to still be considered a girl, and ugly as sin, as far as he was concerned.

And as if that wasn't enough to provoke Calhoun's anger, the fact that the piano player had messed up was the last straw. He had hired the tall, skinny old-timer to play the piano while Lola danced and, instead of paying the fellow cash, he had offered him all the free drinks he wanted during the

165

evening. The fellow had come in an hour before he was to start playing and he was already drunk.

"Where in the hell is the big crowd that was supposed to show up tonight?" Calhoun muttered as he looked toward the batwing doors, expecting a throng of men to stream into the saloon at any minute.

Calhoun was suffering from a bad hangover and he was in no mood to put up with any shit. And yet, everything was starting out all wrong and his head was throbbing with pain.

After Laurette had quit and run off with Bolt the day before, Monte had put the strong drinks away all afternoon until he couldn't stand up. He had stopped drinking late in the day, hoping to sober up enough to look presentable at the saloon during the evening hours when the Prairie Schooner would be crowded. But, it had turned out to be a bad night at the saloon and he had taken up the bottle again after most of his customers walked out when they discovered that Laurette wasn't singing there anymore.

He had suffered through his hangover all day, vowing not to get drunk on Lola's opening night. A half an hour earlier, when he'd realized that there weren't very many customers coming into the Prairie Schooner that night, he'd become so upset that he'd finally allowed himself his first drink of the day. It had been a double shot of whiskey and now he was on his second one of those.

Calhoun was wearing the same gray plaid suit that he'd worn the night Laurette Armand had started singing at his saloon. Because of his dark mood, his shoulders seemed to slope even more than before.

"They'll be along," Ox Jarboe said. "Hell, everybody in town saw that banner. You're bound to draw more customers than this." Jarboe was drinking his usual beer, but he was a big man and the drinks didn't affect him like they did Calhoun.

"Yeah? Well, where in the hell are they?" Calhoun snapped.

"Have a little patience, Monte. They'll be here. It's still early."

"Patience my ass. It's all Bolt's fault, the dirty bastard."

"What's Bolt's fault?"

"Everything. Every damned thing," Calhoun shouted, his face flushed with rage.

"Don't get yourself in a snit, Monte," Jarboe said. "Business will build back up if you give it a chance. If Lola's any good, word will spread fast and you'll fill this place up to the rafters."

"Yeah? Well, so far, I'm not too impressed with Lola," Calhoun said sarcastically, giving his friend a dirty look.

"Why don't we just sit here and watch her performance? Then you decide whether you like her or not," Jarboe said.

Calhoun downed his drink, passed it over to Sam Norris for a refill. He turned toward the stage, his anger brewing deep inside him as he watched the horse-faced woman on the stage.

Lola was anything but graceful as she danced around the stage, waving her arms in slow circles, making suggestive moves that didn't come across.

"Take it off," yelled one of the customers. "Take it

all off."

Others joined the chant.

Lola slipped the kimono down off her shoulders, held it closed so that it covered everything except her bare shoulders. She did a few twirls across the stage, then came back to the middle of the platform. After the rowdy customers whistled for more, she slowly dropped the silk robe to her waist, exposing breasts that had long ago lost their firmness.

Calhoun was sick when he saw Lola's long, sagging breasts. Still, his temper flared when some of the unruly men showed their displeasure of Lola's odd shape by hissing and booing.

Lola quickly dropped the kimono to the floor and danced across the front of the stage in the nude, her pendulous breasts swinging back and forth to the tempo of the music. She was fat and lumpy and when she wiggled her ass, she looked like a pig with an itch on its butt.

"Put it back on!" shouted a crude customer. "Put it all back on."

Laughter rippled through the saloon. Three or four drunken men started yelling the same phrase over and over. "Put it back on, Lola!" Others stomped their feet and booed. A few of the unhappy customers got up and walked out of the saloon, shouting lewd remarks as they went.

"Shit," Calhoun growled. "For chrissakes, Ox, where in the hell did you find that slut?" He tipped his tumbler up and drank a double shot of whiskey down in one gulp. He automatically passed it across the counter to Sam Norris for another refill.

"For what you were willing to pay, that's the best I

could find," Jarboe said. "A dollar a night for parading around in the nude ain't gonna bring you a raving beauty like Laurette. You gotta put some money into it if you expect to make money."

"You could have tried a little harder to find some gal who wasn't over the hill. You could have told some pretty girl that she could make extra money for herself by bedding a few of the customers. You could have done anything but what you did."

"I ain't a pimp, Monte. And don't blame me for your failures. I did the best I could with the money you were willing to pay for a stripper."

The booing and hissing and stomping became too much for Lola and she finally ran off the stage in tears. The piano player, too drunk to know that she was gone, kept right on playing, missing most of the keys as his fingers fumbled across the keyboard.

"Dammit," Calhoun roared, "I've got to get Laurette back here. That's all there is to it. Laurette is the only thing that can save the Prairie Schooner."

"How're you gonna do that, Monte?" Jarboe asked. "You plannin' on riding out to Bolt's place and kidnapping her?"

"That's exactly what we're going to do, Ox," Calhoun said. "Bolt stole Laurette from me and we're gonna steal her right back."

"What's this 'we' shit? I ain't ridin' out there and gettin' my ass shot off over that disloyal bitch. She ain't worth it, Monte."

"I thought you were my friend," Calhoun said sullenly.

"Friend, yes. Stupid, no."

"You're a fuckin' coward," Calhoun roared.

"Maybe so," Jarboe said, "but I ain't ridin' out there with you. You want her back so damned bad, then find somebody else to go with you."

"To hell with you. I'll go by myself."

"It's the booze talkin', Monte," Jarboe said. "If you was sober, you'd realize you couldn't pull it off by yourself."

"I'm not drunk," Calhoun argued. "You'll see when I come back with Laurette." He snatched his Stetson off the counter, paused long enough to drink the whiskey that was in front of him.

"Ox is right, Monte," Norris said. "You shouldn't be riding out there stirring up a fuss with all that liquor in you."

"Don't you tell me what to do, Sam," Calhoun snapped. "I'm the boss here, not you."

"Listen to me, Monte," Norris said calmly. He grabbed Calhoun's arm and kept him from leaving. "Even if you brought Laurette back here, she'd run off again. We talked about this before. You can't force her to stay against her will."

"But I've got to get her back, one way or the other," Calhoun protested, his voice badly slurred. "Otherwise, we're out of business. And if the Prairie Schooner closes, you're out of a job." He tried to jerk his arm free, but was too drunk to have any coordination.

"The only way you're going to get her back is if she comes willin'," Jarboe said. "If you was smart, you'd see to it that she didn't want to work for Bolt anymore. Then she'd come runnin' back to you."

The barkeep released his hold on Monte's arm.

"And how am I going to do that?" Calhoun

swayed against the counter.

"You could send some men out there to ruin her performance," Jarboe suggested. "She wouldn't like it none if things got real rough out there at Bolt's place while she was singin'."

Calhoun thought about it with his whiskey-soaked brain. After a minute, he sneered. "Ox, you're a genius."

"I always thought so," Jarboe said.

Calhoun reached for his tumbler. It was empty. He stared blankly at it for a minute, then turned away from the bar.

"Where're you goin', Monte?" Jarboe asked.

Monte Calhoun fumed as he kicked a chair out of the way, moved to the center of the room in the Prairie Schooner. Men clambered out of his way, saw the anger blossom like a raging flower on his unsmiling face. Gone was his horsetooth smile and his slick look of confidence. So, too, the swagger and the braggadocio. Rather, he looked like he had grown a foot and filled out the shoulders of his gray plaid suit.

"Men, I want your attention," he boomed. "I got me a big problem and I want to pay out some money to any who will give me a hand."

The men in the saloon murmured among themselves. A couple at the bar, who'd had too much to drink, swayed and tried to focus on Monte or his red string tie. Something in his thundering voice jolted them out of their stupor and they straightened up, cocked hands to their ears.

"We're with you, Calhoun," yelled a rowdy across the room. "Just say the word."

"Those sonsofbitches over at the Rocking Bar Bordello have stolen my song bird, the lovely Laurette Armand. I take that mighty personal. You want her back, don't you?"

His question drew a spirited series of cheers and hoorays from the enthusiastic crowd and Calhoun swelled with pride. He knew his men, knew how to work on their emotions. He looked at each one, it seemed, swept them with a hard-boiled glance that told them he meant business. He held up his hands for silence, looking like a scarecrow come to life with his russet hair shining in the lamplight, slightly askew from running worried fingers through the strands on both sides of his middle part.

"I'll pay each man jack of you two dollars to ride over to Bolt's goddamned whorehouse and ruin Laurette's performance tonight. And, I'll buy each one of you a drink when you return and tell me that she left his stage with tears in her pretty French eyes."

Now the cheers rose up in a resounding chorus as the men crowded toward the center of the room, pushing and jostling each other. Calhoun pulled out a wad of single dollar bills, plucked fresh from the safe in his office. He held the stack of notes up high so every man there could see the green of them, hear the crispness as he fanned them like a deck of cards.

"That's gonna cost Mister Calhoun a pretty penny," said a man still standing at the bar.

"It's an easy two dollars," said the bartender. "And a free drink besides."

"Hell, I can use two buckskins," said the man, and he quaffed the remainder of his drink and joined the throng. Calhoun began peeling off dollar bills, two at a time and the men clutched them, started out the door, a long line of them, eager to descend on the Rocking Bar Bordello and raise a little hell. Some carried their bottles with them, and some tucked the bills in their pockets as if afraid they would fly away.

Calhoun finished paying the last man. The room was very nearly empty. He swelled up, bloated with satisfaction.

"Now," he said, "let's see how Bolt likes it when the tables are turned. I'll have Laurette back here by tomorrow night and we'll put that damned pimp out of business."

There was no one there to argue the point with Monte Calhoun and he strode to the bar for another drink, a smirk smeared across his face like a bright new flag.

CHAPTER FOURTEEN

The two-dollar men started arriving at the Rocking Bar just before Laurette was due to appear on the small stage. There was an air of expectancy among the patrons, but when the bleary-eyed claque of men began strutting into the saloon, Tom Penrod heard warning Klaxons sound in his brain.

"Bolt, you see what I see?"

"Looks like a pretty good crowd, Tom."

"Trouble, maybe."

Bolt laughed, finally feeling more relaxed. He and Tom stood at the far end of the bar, watching the place fill up. The talk was low and easy, all eyes watching the stage, listening to the small group of musicians tune up. Tom had a single candle lit in front of the closed stage curtain so that it threw a faint glow on the place where the French *chanteuse* would make her entrance in just a few moments.

"Tom, those are just Laurette's well-wishers, men who drank over there at Calhoun's before coming to listen to their favorite songbird. We'll do some bang-up business here tonight."

"Yeah, I recognize some of those jaspers. Maybe you're right. It just looks funny, that's all. All of 'em comin' in here at one time."

"They probably asked for Laurette over at the Prairie Schooner and found out she was here. Relax. Enjoy the evening."

Bolt turned to his drink, lifted it to his lips. The orchestra stopped tuning up. The leader tapped his violin bow on a music stand and a hush fell over the room. One of Bolt's men lit the remaining candles that served as footlights.

The band hit a chord, then struck up a lively fanfare. The curtains slowly parted and Laurette stepped into the glow of the footlights. Chet, holding onto a lantern with flat, mirrored flanges, stood on a ladder to one side, directing the beam onto Laurette's face.

The orchestra changed pitch, went into a minor key, vamped the lead-in to a torchy French love song. There wasn't a sound in the room as she opened her mouth to sing.

She sang the first few notes, her dulcet tones caressing the French words, *l'amour, toujours, l'amour,* and Bolt leaned back against the bar top, a look of satisfaction spreading across his face. Laurette looked beautiful, stunning in the soft light. Her delicate face shone in the lamplight's beam and her smile was as dazzling as white clouds floating in a blue sky over the mountains.

Laurette was halfway through her opening song when the first of the rowdies stood up, shook his fist at the songstress and began to boo. Another got to his feet and hissed loudly at her. The others in the claque joined in, some of them stomping their feet on the floor.

"Goddamn!" shouted Penrod and jumped away from the bar before Bolt could stop him.

Laurette tried gamely to continue her song, but the orchestra began to break up, the lead fiddler's bow screeching on a series of off-key notes. Someone threw a bottle at the drummer and it bounced off the rim of his snare and crashed onto the small stage. Laurette cried out and backed away.

Tom grabbed the nearest troublemaker and drew back his fist. He shot a straight right to the man's temple, struck him hard. The man staggered into another, his eyes glazed, rolled back in their sockets. He went down like a sack of meal and one of the rowdies yelled and waded into Tom, his fists swinging like the blades of a windmill.

Bolt hurtled away from the bar and rushed into the fray. Men rose to their feet and began pummeling one another, kicking, throwing clenched fists at the nearest man, regardless of his sympathies. The fight erupted into a free-for-all as shouting, angry men picked up chairs, crashed into tables, fought for the sheer joy of it.

Bolt grabbed a man by the collar, turned him around and threw a hard right to his chin. He heard the crack of his knuckles on bone and watched the man stagger backwards into another man holding a chair high above his head.

Hysteria gripped the mob. Some of the women, who had been watching the performance from the sidelines, screamed and began running for cover.

The bartenders joined the wild fray, one of them swinging a bung starter at a trio of men locked in combat. Tom took a fist in the stomach and felt the air rush from his lungs. He doubled over, fighting down the bile that rose in his throat.

A mass of men surged back and forth, fighting hard, and Bolt danced out of their way, pumping his fists into a man's back, slashing at his kidneys with pile-driving one-two punches. A large man threw a bottle at Bolt. He ducked just in time, but felt a boot smash into his shin. Pain shot up his leg and he saw red. He ring-necked the man and wrestled him to the floor as a fist crashed into his ribs.

Tom felt a blow rocket off his cheekbone. Stars danced in the temporary darkness of his brain and he whirled, struck out blindly, hitting a red-faced man swinging a broken chair leg. One of the patrons went flying past him, hit a table and shattered it to splinters.

The mass of men flowed to-and-fro like a tide and it no longer was a question of who was on which side. There was fighting to be done and fists shot out blindly, striking friends and hostiles alike.

Bolt was doing his damnedest to sort it all out, to make his way through the packed mob and find Laurette, see if she was all right. Every time he got to his feet, someone knocked him down. Most of the time, it was just one man shoving another. There was no longer any particular person to fight, to knock down. The mob had its own brain and it was dumb to reason.

Bolt saw Tom Penrod with his arms around the necks of a pair of men, trying to crack their heads together like eggs. Tom was grinning like a shit-eating dog, having the time of his life. The last he saw of him, Tom went down as a bunch of men surged toward him like a giant wave of muscled arms and thick skulls. His yell was drowned out among the others who shouted at full voice.

Bolt shouldered his way through the crowd, ducking, striking out when someone blocked his way. He finally made it to the stage and drew his pistol. He cocked it, pointed it in the air. He pulled the trigger. The shot boomed and a cloud of white smoke belched from the barrel.

"Enough!" shouted Bolt. "I'll shoot the next man who throws a punch."

The din died down. The men on the floor looked up at Bolt, who now held the pistol leveled at his side, a thin plume of smoke curling from the snout of the barrel. Bolt glanced around and picked out one of the men he had seen drinking at the Schooner, gestured with his pistol.

"You," he said tersely, "get up."

Sheepishly, the man rose to his feet.

"Who put you up to this?" asked Bolt.

The man hung his head, looking down at his boots.

"I want an answer quick," said Bolt, "or you'll be carried out of here on a board."

"Calhoun—he—he paid us to raise some cain."

"How much?"

"Two dollars."

"And a free drink!" yelled another man.

Bolt's face turned to granite. The anger boiled up inside him and his eyes flashed with flint and steel.

He swept the crowd with a scathing glance and some would say later they saw his finger curl around the trigger and they were sure he would shoot someone, anyone, dead, if anyone so much as breathed.

"You bastards get out of here," he said tightly, "and get your free drinks. Get out now, every one of you who took Monte Calhoun up on his cheap offer. I'm going to start shooting after I count to ten."

Men scrambled to their feet. Some, already standing, broke from the crowd and ran to the door, disappeared into the darkness outside. Bolt watched them go, more than a dozen men, and he fired another shot into the air just to put some git in their britches.

Tom rose from the floor, shook himself off and began dusting his trousers. He had a lump on one cheek, a thin trickle of blood running at the corner of his mouth. He smiled wanly at Bolt.

Those patrons who had been there before went to the bar and some started putting the tables and chairs back in order.

"Pretty good fight," grinned Tom.

Bolt was not amused.

"Tom, just shut up," he said softly. "Get yourself a drink."

"Hell, Jared, I didn't start nothin'."

Bolt shot him a withering look, slammed his pistol back in its holster. He turned on his heel and stalked through the curtains, looking for Laurette. When he didn't find her in the kitchen or the dining room, he headed out the back door and ran toward her cottage. His anger began to subside by the time he knocked on her door.

"Laurette, it's me, Bolt," he called out.

"Go away," she cried.

"Laurie, I want to talk to you. Let me in."

"No. Just go away and leave me alone."

"Please, Laurie," he begged. "I need to explain to you what happened."

After a minute, he heard the inside bolt scrape across the metal that held it in place. The door opened and Laurette stood there, an angry look on her face.

"May I come in?" Bolt asked.

"Not for long," she said.

Bolt went in and closed the door.

Laurette stood there, her arms folded across her chest.

"Laurie, I'm sorry about what happened over there," he said.

"I hope you are," she said sarcastically. "I told you I didn't want to work in a bordello. Now you know why."

"But, Laurie . . ."

"You attract crude, boorish patrons with your house of sin. You lied to me, Bolt. You told me that all of the men who come here had to act like gentlemen. You said you'd toss them out if they caused trouble."

"But, Laurie . . ." Bolt tried again, but he couldn't get the words out before she interrupted.

"If you think those crude fellows over there were acting like gentlemen, then you and I disagree on what the word means."

"Laurie, please listen to me."

"I listened to you before. I believed you, Bolt. I

trusted you. But, no more."

"Laurie, I didn't know those men were coming or I'd have stopped them at the door and sent them packing."

"It doesn't matter. Whorehouses attract rough, crude, vicious, brawling men, if you can call them that, and I won't stand for it. You give up your whores and go legitimate or I won't work for you anymore."

"I won't do that, Laurie," Bolt said calmly, although he was raging with anger inside. How dare she suggest such a thing? "I'm sorry, but my girls deserve my loyalty."

"Loyalty? Hah!"

"I promised my girls a home and I promised them jobs, and I'm not going back on my word."

"If you'd rather have prostitutes working for you instead of me, then that's your choice," Laurette said haughtily. "I'll leave in the morning and I'll take Ken and Cherie with me."

"Laurie, will you please listen to me for a minute?" Bolt said, his anger diminishing. "Those men who caused the trouble over there weren't regular customers of mine. They were sent here by Monte Calhoun with the express purpose of ruining your performance. Calhoun paid them to cause trouble while you were singing so that you would get mad enough to quit your job here and go running back to him."

Laurette's expression softened. "Monte paid them to start trouble? That's outrageous."

"Monte's outrageous. You ought to know that by now."

"Well, I certainly wouldn't go running back to him for a job, no matter what. But, Bolt, I can't work under these conditions—never knowing if there's going to be trouble."

"I understand that, Laurie. I'll make it up to you somehow."

"There's no way you can make it up to me now, Bolt," she said. "What's done is done and you can't take it back."

"No, I guess not, but I can make sure it never happens again."

"How can you guarantee it? You can't."

"I'll hire some men of my own to keep the roughnecks out. I'll put some men out by the front entrance, too. We won't let any of Calhoun's men get near the bordello."

"Monte is persistent. He'll send more men," Laurette argued. She toyed nervously with the necklace around her neck. "What if they are armed? The thought of being involved in a shootout scares me to death. I just couldn't work under such tense conditions."

"You won't have to. My men will be armed. Besides stationing guards at the entrance, I'll surround the bordello with men. Calhoun's men won't set foot on my property."

"If you still allow men to patronize the bordello, then you can't be absolutely sure that those men who do come inside the bordello aren't really someone hired by Monte, can you?" Laurette said, reasoning aloud. "Not unless you personally know every single person you let in here. And I doubt that that's the case."

"We'll have every man check his weapon as he comes in the door. And we'll have enough men inside the bordello so that, if anyone starts anything, he'll be properly pounced on. I assure you, Laurie, there's no way I'm going to allow you to be put in any kind of a dangerous situation. You have my word on it and that's the only thing I can guarantee."

"If you do all those things, it sounds like the bordello will be secure enough," she said. "I will stay on, but if there is ever any more trouble, I will leave immediately, even if Ken and Cherie and I have to borrow your buggy and leave in the middle of the night."

"I'm sure there won't be any more trouble," Bolt said. "Monte will get the message when his men return to the Prairie Schooner tonight to collect their free drinks."

"And, knowing Monte, they won't get the free drinks just for their effort," Laurie said with a half smile. "Monte wants results. Immediate results."

"I think you're right." Bolt smiled.

Laurette rushed into his arms, wrapped her own around his waist. "Oh, Bolt, I was so frightened. Please hold me tight."

Bolt put his arms around Laurette and pulled her up close against him, held her tight for a long time. Finally, when she looked up at him, he lowered his head and kissed her gently on the lips. She responded with a passion that burned his lips, a passion that seared his loins with its heat and caused his shaft to start growing. Suddenly he wanted her so much, he couldn't think of anything else.

Bolt slid his hand up across the smooth fabric of

her soft gown. Just as he touched the covered mound of her breast, Laurette broke the kiss. She was quivering when she backed away from him.

"You'd better go now, Bolt," she said, the ache of desire evident in the husk of her velvet voice.

"I don't want to go," he said.

"I know, but it's best that you do," she said, a sadness in her eyes. "Please, Bolt, before something happens that we'll both regret."

Bolt took in a deep breath, let it out slowly, trying to quell his passion, his needs. He wanted to tell her that he wouldn't regret anything they did together. He wanted to tell her how beautiful she was, how irresistible she was, but he wouldn't push it. Not now. Maybe not ever.

He knew, though, that the next time they were alone together, there was a chance that neither one of them could stay their twin passions before they went to the point of no return.

CHAPTER FIFTEEN

Monte Calhoun was furious when the hired men came back with nothing more for their efforts than bruised bodies. Each man told the same story. Laurette had run off stage when the trouble started, but they were all sure that Bolt would be able to convince her to stay. The men reported that, somehow, Bolt had found out that Calhoun had hired them to cause trouble during Laurette's performance, but not a single man would tell him how Bolt found out. They all claimed total ignorance.

The following night, Monte Calhoun sent a dozen more men, different men this time, out to the Rocking Bar Ranch to spoil Laurette's performance. Same offer. Two dollars and a free drink when they got back. Before they headed out to Bolt's ranch, he told them to give the singer a good scare if they could. He was getting desperate. His money was about to run out and he needed the Prairie Schooner to start paying off fast. Besides, he didn't like the idea of Laurette being around Bolt all the time.

When that group of men came back to collect their drinks, their report was even grimmer than that of the night before. Calhoun was sitting at the bar with Ox Jarboe. There were not more than a dozen men in the place. Lola had run off that first night after being embarrassed and she never did come back to collect her dollar.

"Hell, they've got armed guards crawling all over the place out there," reported one of the men as the riders walked over to the end of the bar where Calhoun and Jarboe were sitting. "Joe was the only one who got inside the bordello."

"Yeah," said a tall, slim man. "When we saw those guards at the entrance to Bolt's property, we stopped before they spotted us comin'. Half of us circled around and went in across the pasture while the other half stayed out on the road."

"Didn't do us no good," said a man with a limp. "Bolt's got that damned bordello ringed with guards. No way anybody's gonna get in there."

"How did Joe get in, then?" Calhoun asked.

"We all backed way off and discussed our predicament," said the man with the limp. "We decided that Joe had a chance of getting in if he went by himself. He looked better than the rest of us."

Calhoun glanced around. "Where is Joe?" he asked.

"He was shot," said the tall, slim man.

"Killed?" Calhoun shook his head.

"No, but he's in pretty tough shape," said the first man. "We dropped him off at the sawbones on our way into town."

"The doc says he'll live," said the tall one, "but he'll sure in hell never use his shootin' arm again."

"Damn!" Calhoun said. "Anything else I should know?"

"Only that Laurette is still singing at the Rocking Bar," said the one with a limp. "Joe said she looked quite content out there."

"How'd they get Joe?" Calhoun asked.

"Joe said he got past the entrance guards because they thought he was just a customer," said another man. "Joe went through the guards at the house the same way, claiming he was there to pay for the pleasures of one of the whores. But when he got inside, they told him he had to check his gun. Joe refused."

The man who limped spoke up. "If Joe had just gone along with them and checked that damned gun, nobody would have suspected a thing. Joe'd be here right now telling you about it.

"When he refused to give up his pistol, somebody got suspicious. Joe got scared and bolted out the door. Luckily, it took the guards a couple of minutes to figure out what was going on. Joe was halfway to the hitching post where he'd tied his horse when someone came out of the house and said to stop him.

"Three or four guards shot at him," Limpy said. "We heard the shots. Joe took off across the dark fields and we caught up with him down the road a spell when he circled back onto the main road."

"Dammit, we'll probably never get in there now. They won't fall for the same trick twice," Calhoun said, showing no concern for the wounded man.

"Not unless you send unarmed men in one at a time," the thin one said, "and I sure as hell ain't goin' out there again."

"Neither am I," said another.

"Go on and get your free drinks," Calhoun said, disgusted with all of them.

The eleven men scampered to the other end of the bar and ordered their drinks. Most of them would spend their two dollars on additional drinks, so Monte wouldn't be out very much money in the long run.

"What're you gonna do now, Monte?" Jarboe asked.

"Well, I've got an idea," Calhoun said, his mind spinning with a new scheme. "You interested?"

"Without even asking what it is, I think I'll pass," Ox said. He took a sip of beer and didn't bother to look over at Calhoun.

"I want Bolt out of the picture," Calhoun said with a cold, calculating tone to his voice.

"You mean permanently, or just until you can get Laurette out of there?"

"I mean I want him turned into buzzard bait."

Ox turned and looked at Monte to see if he was serious. "Jesus, you're talking murder."

"That's right."

"Forget it, Monte. It's not one of your better plans," Ox said casually, unable to believe that Calhoun could actually plot someone's murder. Monte was a swindler, a cheat, and probably a lot of other things, and he'd even killed a few men. But not cold-blooded murder, as far as he knew. "There ain't no gal in the world worth havin' that kind of thing on your conscience for the rest of your life."

"It wouldn't bother me," Calhoun said. "And I don't give a fuck about getting Laurette back anymore. I just want Bolt dead."

"Why? Are you jealous because he's got a bordello and you don't?"

Jarboe's words struck a sore spot in Calhoun's festering, sick mind. Monte wasn't about to admit it, but that's exactly why he hated Bolt. Bolt was a success, he wasn't. It was that simple. Monte had spent all of his life trying to prove to his father that he was strong and successful and, even though his father had been dead six years now, he was still trying to prove it.

"It don't matter. I'll pay you two hundred dollars to do the job."

Ox Jarboe laughed. "You're barkin' up the wrong tree, Monte. I ain't a killer."

"I'll make you a partner in the Prairie Schooner," Calhoun said. "I know that's what you've been wanting for a long time."

Ox gave Calhoun a long, hard look. "If I wanted to be a partner, I'd buy my way in with hard cash, Monte, not with another man's life."

"Nobody would know," Calhoun begged.

"I would know," Ox said. "After living in the mountains for so long and facing death so many times, I've got a healthy respect for a man's life. Any man's life. And that includes Bolt."

"I didn't think you liked Bolt."

"I don't, but I ain't gonna kill him. Only two things would make me kill a man."

"What two things?" Monte asked, an expression

of hope on his face.

"One is if a man's fixin' to pull the trigger of a gun that's pointed at me and the other is if someone's fixin' to shoot a friend of mine in the back. You'll have to get someone else to do your dirty work, Monte, and I think you've already used up all the fellows around here who could help you out."

"Are you sayin' I should hire an outside gun?" Calhoun said.

"I ain't sayin' anything," Ox said. "I'm just tellin' you I don't want no part of murder."

"Do you know a fellow named Lew Badham?" Monte asked.

"No, and I don't want to know him," Ox said. "I don't want to hear any more about it, Monte. You're just havin' pipe dreams 'cause you're mad at the whole damned world."

"Not at the whole world, Ox. Just a couple of people. I'm gonna see this thing through."

"I think it's the booze in you that's doin' the talkin' again," Jarboe said. "The other night you was so staggerin'-ass drunk, you didn't even remember nothin' about it the next mornin'. I think you'd better lay off the hooch until you can get your thinkin' all cleared up."

"You don't believe me, do you, Ox?"

"I told ya, Monte, I don't want to talk about it anymore." Ox Jarboe picked his hat up off the counter, slid it onto his thick head of hair. "I'll see you tomorrow. Maybe you'll be feelin' better in the mornin'." He turned and walked away without finishing his beer.

Monte Calhoun watched his friend go. So Ox

didn't believe him. Well, he'd show him that he could accomplish what he set out to do.

Sam Norris had been busy serving the free drinks to the loud fellows at the other end of the bar. He hadn't heard any of Monte's conversation, but he figured something was wrong. Monte Calhoun looked wild-eyed as he stared into his empty glass. Another thing, Ox Jarboe usually didn't leave this early in the evening and, as long as Sam had known Ox, he'd never known the big mountain man to leave a single drop of beer in his glass. Jarboe had too much Scotch blood for that.

"Are you all right?" Sam said as he looked at Monte.

"I've never been better," Calhoun said. "Give me another drink, Sam."

Sam knew that Monte had had enough whiskey to make him good and drunk. However, Calhoun was not acting drunk. No slurred speech as far as he could tell. No wavering on the stool like he usually did. Only that wild, faraway look in his eyes.

"I think you've had enough, Monte. I don't want you hurtin' yourself."

"Give me a drink, Sam," Calhoun insisted. "I'm about to get my whole life straightened out."

CHAPTER SIXTEEN

Lew Badham knew how to earn his money. He had done this many times before. He could call a coward out and goad the man into going for hardware, knowing he hadn't a snowball's chance in hell of beating Lew to the draw.

He stood at the bar of the Prairie Schooner, letting the patrons get a good look at him. He was tall, lean, slim-hipped, with arms like whips, dark hair that hung straight from his Montana-creased Stetson, a face that looked as if it had been hacked square with a double-bitted axe. The high cheekbones guarded his hazel eyes, eyes that were brown as nuts, flecked with yellow and green, piercing without revealing anything of the inner man. Monte Calhoun had hired him and he meant to earn his pay, but he was his own man and he knew how to ply his trade.

Badham stood with one foot on the brass rail, a drink in his hand, his back to the bar. He looked at the patrons as if they were not there. That is, he looked right through them, yet gave each man the uncomfortable feeling that he alone was skewered by that scathing, contemptuous glance from those cold, green-gold, nut-brown eyes.

"Heard you got yourself a whore a-singin' songs in this saloon," Badham said loudly, and every man there froze and focused his attention on the tall stranger at the bar. "Some French slut that spreads her legs for a pint-sized, little pianner player name of Selves. What's her name? Laurette?"

"We don't hold with talkin' about wimmin in the saloon," said a man who had had too much to drink. "'Specially not Miss Laurette."

Badham didn't want this man. But he could serve his purpose as well as any.

"You got whores here, don't you? Well, this French canary's same as any gal o' the line I seen in Hays, Abilene, Fort Worth or Taos. Whores ain't women, no how."

"Laurette ain't no whore!" shouted the man. Someone told him to shut up.

"I say Laurette's a whore," said Badham, a bemused smile flickering on his lips. "She and that pianner player pimp of hers ain't fit to 'sociate with decent folks. Anybody here say different?"

Even the drunk kept his mouth shut. Badham turned his back on the whole bunch, lifted his drink to his lips. A moment later, a man named Barney Huddleston slipped out of the door of the saloon, his face red, his chest full to bursting. He knew where to spread the news of the gunslinger's slurring remarks about Laurette and Ken Selves. A few moments later, he was laying leather to his horse and flying toward Bolt's Rocking Bar Ranch.

Lew Badham finished his drink and sat at a table in the corner of the saloon with a bottle and a glass. Now, all that remained was to wait for Bolt to come after him. He knew he could never get to the man on his own ranch. One of Badham's rules was to always get his man away from where he felt at home. Get him on ground that Lew claimed for his own.

Lew Badham had chosen the Prairie Schooner as home ground. This was where he would kill Bolt.

Barney Huddleston rode up to Bolt's, his horse in a lather. He called out. No one answered. He lit down, wrapped the reins around the hitchrail and stalked into the bordello.

Ken Selves sat at the piano, picking out a few chords. They resonated in the empty room, tinkled like glass shards. Barney saw him in the dimness, walked toward him.

"Where's Bolt?"

"I have no idea," said Ken.

"Looky," said Huddleston, "there's one mean jasper in town makin' talk about Miss Armand. And you, too, Selves."

Ken spun around on the stool, his delicate hands still poised in midair.

"Who are you?"

"Name's Barney Huddleston. I seen you play for Miss Armand. Heard her sing, too. Right purty. She ain't no whore, I know that."

"What did you say?" asked Ken, an edge to his voice like a fine-honed razor.

"Wasn't me what said it, but that owlhooter over to the Schooner. Name of Lew Badham. He says Miss Armand's a whore. Called you a pimp, too."

Ken rose from the piano stool, walked over to Huddleston. He looked him over carefully.

"Somebody put you up to this?" he asked.

"No. I come on my own. Figgered Bolt would want to hear this slander firsthand. I just come from the Schooner."

"I haven't seen Bolt," said Selves, "but this doesn't concern him."

"Huh?"

"I'll take care of Mister Badham."

"You? Why that man's ten kinds of mean and wears a hogleg on his hip that would make you swaller your Adam's apple. You better stay out of this."

Ken appeared very calm. He was calm. He looked at Huddleston with steady eyes, eyes that were shadowing up with a terrible anger deep inside him. Huddleston winced under the onslaught of the gaze.

"You ride back to that saloon, Mister Huddleston, and tell Mister Badham that I'll be in directly to speak to him about his slander concerning Miss Armand."

"You goin' up agin' Badham alone?"

"You tell him I'll be there." Selves turned Huddleston around, patting him on the back, between the shoulders. He nudged Huddleston toward the door.

"I won't be long," said Selves softly. "Tell Mister Badham to wait for me."

"Jesus Christ," muttered Huddleston. "I'm sorry I

ome out now. There's gonna be a killin' for sure."

"Yes," said Ken, and he walked away, headed for the bunkhouse. Huddleston watched him go, then mounted up. He rode back to town a lot more slowly than he had come out.

Ken opened the theatrical trunk in the bunkhouse. He was shocked, angered that Badham had called Laurette a whore. He didn't care what they said about him, but her honor was at stake. He would not say anything to her. He wouldn't insult her by sullying her ears with such trash.

He dug through his trunk, sighed when he found the pistol wrapped in oilcloth. He picked up a box of ammunition, closed the trunk. He unwrapped the pistol, checked its action. The pistol was small, a Smith & Wesson .32, nickel-plated. He cracked it open, fed five bullets into the cylinder. He stuck the pistol in his waistband, stalked from the bunkhouse.

Ken was no stranger to the gun. He had been in the war and he knew how to kill. He had been decorated for bravery when he fought with the infantry, the 2nd Illinois. But he had told himself, when the war was over, that he would never kill again. The pistol, however, was something he carried with him because he knew, deep down, that men could not be trusted. He had hoped never to have to fight again, but there was no getting out of this. If he did not stand up for Laurette, then he would not be able to live with himself.

He had been decorated for bravery under fire and that was no accident. Ken Selves was not a man to shirk his responsibility. Despite his gentle nature, he had never backed away from a fight.

It took him only a few moments to saddle a horse. He rode into town with a heavy heart, but his conscience was clear. If Badham's words were allowed to stand unchallenged, then people might begin to believe the slander. Ken wouldn't allow that to happen. Even if it cost him his life.

The street was quiet when Ken rode up to the Prairie Schooner. Ominously quiet. A man's face at the front window suddenly disappeared and Ken knew that Badham would soon know that he was here. He did not know the man, but he was probably waiting inside—if his message had been delivered.

Ken slid out of the saddle, dusted himself off, straightened his hat, his tie. He polished the toes of his boots by rubbing them on the back of his trouser legs. Then, he walked through the batwing doors like a man with a purpose. He strode into the bar, slapped down a cartwheel.

"I'll have a drink," said Ken to the bartender. "Straight whiskey."

"Didn't know you drank."

"This is a farewell drink," said Ken.

"You goin' somewhere?"

"Maybe. I meant a farewell to a man named Badham. He here?"

"Over yonder," said the bartender dryly. He poured the drink, snatched up the dollar and went to the far end of the bar. Men cleared a path between Badham's table and the spot where Ken Selves stood at the bar.

Ken lifted the drink, turned to look at the man across the room.

"Mister Badham?"

"I'm Badham. Who are you, Shorty?"

"Ken Selves. I am the piano player for Miss Armand."

"You mean that whore's little pimp, don't you?"

Ken downed the drink, placed the empty glass very carefully on the bar top. He opened his coat, revealed the gleaming nickel of the Smith & Wesson in his waistband.

"You retract those foul accusations, sir," said Ken evenly. "There is not a word of truth to them. Laurette Armand is a lady, and you, sir, are no gentleman. You are a cad and a scoundrel for sullying her good name."

Badham shoved the table away from him with a screech of wooden legs, slammed his chair backwards into the wall. He stood, legs wide apart, hand hovering over the butt of his low-slung pistol.

"You callin' me names, Pimp?"

"I'm calling you what you are, Badham."

Lew Badham laughed, but his eyes never left Ken's face. He laughed and then cut it off short.

A silence grew in the room, grew into something you could almost touch. It was a heavy, ominous silence like the moments in a man's heart, before he joined in battle, when he was alone with only his own thoughts and a prayer to his maker on his lips. It was the kind of silence that haunts the Boot Hill graveyards and the crosses that litter the prairie along the Oregon Trail. It was a silence that turned black as night even in the glaring light of day.

"Jesus," someone whispered, and it was no prayer, but a fearful oath escaping from a man's constricted throat.

"Open the ball, Selves," said Badham as he hunkered into a fighting crouch. "One of us is going to dance."

"Don't do it, Ken," said a man nearby. "You're no match for him.

Ken's lips were dry, but he gave no sign that he had any fear. Every man there looked at him intently, wondering if he was drunk or a fool, or just plain crazy. But Selves stood there calmly, just the trace of a bitter smile on his lips, his back straight, his head held high. He looked at Badham without flinching and the saloon patrons gave him credit for that.

Ken's right hand moved, and some said he brought it down like he did when he played the piano. It was a delicate hand, and now it moved like a bird in flight, down, down toward the Smith & Wesson in his waistband. Every man jack there watched him go for his weapon and every one of them agonized over his slowness. His hand just kept going down and down toward that pistol butt like a stricken bird, looking like a sculpture moving through water, slow, slow, too slow.

Only the bartender looked at Badham. He was the only one who saw Lew's hand streak toward his Colt so fast that it blurred. His hand was like a shadow thrown by a diving hawk. One moment it was suspended in air, the next it was grasping the butt of that Colt and drawing the pistol smooth from the leather, the sound no more than a delicate whisper and an eternity caught in that split second it took to cock the hammer back on the rise.

The pistol seemed to buck in Badham's hand long

before the explosion. Orange flame and a blast of white smoke belched from the snout of the Colt and the pistol bucked again in the outlaw's hand and again. The bartender's gaze darted to Ken quickly. He saw the pianist shudder and twitch, saw the dark hole in the center of his shirt, the spray of pink blood flying out of the fist-sized hole in his back. Ken's body drove back against the bar and hung there as the second bullet caught him just above his waistband, and then a third bullet smashed him in the throat and blood spewed out all over the mirror at the backbar.

Ken, miraculously, came up with the pistol in his hand. The nickel-plating gleamed hideously in the light. He pointed it at Badham and then his mouth bubbled over with a gush of crimson blood. His eyes rolled back in their sockets and he sagged against the bar, slid slowly downward. The pistol fell from his hand, struck a brass spittoon and clattered around for a second or two.

Later, one man said that Ken drew his pistol slower than an inebriated snail, but he gave the man credit for trying. Now, Badham came out of his crouch and popped open the loading gate on his Colt, worked the ejection lever. Empty hulls spanged on the tabletop and he fed fresh cartridges into the empty cylinders.

"One less pimp," he growled, "but there's still another to go. That motherhumping Bolt is the one I want."

No man said a word.

The silence returned, but it was a different silence this time. It was a silence spawned full-blown out of fear and confusion, a silence that was borne on the wings of death and full of emptiness and sadness and the certainty of man's mortality and the grave waiting, inevitably, for every man there that day in the Prairie Schooner.

It was the silence of a man's spilled blood, a blood that no longer ran in the veins, but only on a sawdust floor. It was even now turning dark and hard in little grimy pools where Ken Selves stared sightlessly down at them, his eyes frosted over with the final glaze of death.

CHAPTER SEVENTEEN

Bolt and Tom had been out in the back forty tending to the cattle all morning and part of the early afternoon. They didn't know anything was wrong until they walked into the parlor of the bordello and saw Laurette and Cherie and the six harlots huddled together on the two facing sofas.

Bolt's heart sank and beside him, Tom let out a sound that sounded like a gasp.

The girls had their arms entwined around each other, four on one sofa and four on the other one. There wasn't a dry eye among them. Laurette and Cherie appeared to be wracked with shoulder-jerking sobs. They sat together, with Doreen next to Laurette and Cathy Boring on the other side of Cherie.

"What's the matter?" Bolt asked. He dashed to the sofa, kneeled down in front of Laurette. "Are you hurt?"

Laurette looked at him through a haze of tears. She tried to speak, but nothing intelligible came out of her quivering mouth. Cherie said something in French, but Bolt couldn't understand it.

"Ken's dead," Doreen said, sniffing. Tears rolled down her cheeks and dripped onto her dress. She didn't bother to wipe them away and only dabbed at her runny nose.

Bolt was too stunned to speak for a moment. He took Laurette's hands in his and held them.

Cherie jumped up from the couch and ran to Tom's outstretched arms. He walked her a few feet away from the other women and she felt safe in his arms. She knew she didn't have to say anything for Tom to understand her grief.

"I'm sorry, Laurette," Bolt said gently. He squeezed her hands.

Cathy and Doreen got up right away to make more room on the couch for Bolt. Bolt sat down next to Laurette and put his arm around her shoulder. She snuggled into the crook of his arm and began sobbing all over again.

Bolt looked up at Doreen. "What happened?"

"Ken was murdered," Doreen said, barely able to speak.

"Where?" Tom asked. "Was he out in the bunkhouse?"

"We should have kept guards on around the clock," Bolt said quietly.

"No." Doreen shook her head. "Ken was killed in town, at the bar of the Prairie Schooner saloon."

Bolt's eyebrows shot up. His first thought was Monte Calhoun. He glanced over at Tom and saw the frown burrowed across Tom's forehead.

"What was Ken doing in town?" Tom asked, still holding Cherie in his arms.

"We don't know," Doreen said, dabbing at her nose again. "He had no reason to go to town unless he just felt like it."

"Didn't he tell you he was leaving?"

"We weren't here when he left," Doreen said. "The girls wanted to learn how to ride a horse so they could surprise you, so all of us rode over to the river. We were gone about two hours. Ken was practicing the piano when we left. When we got back, we thought he was over in the bunkhouse resting up for tonight."

"How'd you find out about Ken?" Bolt asked.

"A fellow rode out here to see you about a half an hour ago," Doreen said, trying to compose herself. "He said he needed to talk to you, and although he didn't want to tell us, he finally gave us the news about Ken when he found out that you might not be back until late."

"Did you know him?"

"He said his name was Barney Huddleston."

"Doesn't sound familiar," Tom said.

"What'd he say?" Bolt asked.

"Just that Ken had been murdered at the saloon by a man named Lew Badham." Doreen drew in a breath, tried to stop her voice from quivering. "He said he didn't know any more than that, but I think he was holding something back. It just doesn't make sense."

"I don't know the name Lew Badham," Bolt said after he thought a minute. "Do you, Tom?"

"No, I don't think I've ever heard it before."

"Doreen, can you girls take care of Laurie and Cherie?" Bolt asked. "Tom and I are going to town."

"Yes," Doreen said.

Bolt turned back to Laurette, hugged her tight. "Laurie, we're going to find Ken's killer. Will you be all right?"

Laurette nodded to Bolt and managed a trace of a sad smile.

Bolt and Tom left right away, not even taking time to wash their dirty hands. They both felt that Calhoun was behind Ken's murder, so they avoided the Prairie Schooner. They stopped at another watering hole in town and were surprised to see so many men in there that early in the day.

As they walked to the bar, Bolt overheard one old duffer tell another that the Prairie Schooner was cursed now and that he'd never go inside again. Not as long as he lived. Bolt paused just long enough to hear the other old-timer say that he didn't believe in curses, but that he'd never go in the Prairie Schooner, either. He said that he'd never be able to walk through those batwing doors without seeing that poor piano player's bloody body lying on the floor.

Ken's death was the talk of the town. Bolt and Tom talked to several men at the first saloon, then went to another one for awhile. They heard several versions of the story, but there were certain things that were consistent in each telling of Ken's death.

"They all said Ken was drunk," Tom said on the ride back to the ranch. "Some of them swore they saw Ken take a drink at the Prairie Schooner."

"I know, it doesn't make sense. Laurette said he

never drank."

"He always turned down wine at supper and I never saw him take a drink in the bordello when he was working."

"They all said he challenged Lew Badham," Bolt said, puzzled by it all.

"Some said Ken drew on Badham," Tom said.

"And Laurette has said that Ken won't fight."

"Hell, the first time we ever saw Ken, he was running away from a fight."

"Yeah," Bolt said, "and as far as I knew, Ken didn't own a gun, yet they claim he was armed. I guess we should have gone to the Schooner to see if Badham was there, but since everybody said Ken drew first, not much we could do about it."

When the two men got home, the girls were still in the parlor. Laurette wasn't sobbing, but she was grief-stricken. Bolt told her everything he knew.

"Ken would not hurt a fly," Laurette said, suddenly angered. "Even if he is called bad names, he swallows it. He was an artist. He composed most of my songs and he was my trusted friend."

"But everyone said that he made the challenge and that he drew first," Bolt said.

"No, someone made him do what he did," Laurette said. "Ken did not drink and that old pistol of his was what he carried in the war."

"I didn't know he had a gun," Bolt said.

"Yes. Ken was a very brave man and he was honored for his heroism. But when the war was over, Ken vowed he would never kill again. He kept that old pistol to remind him of his sacred vow. He also carried his war decorations in that trunk. And his medals and commendations for bravery. I have always told you that Ken was a very brave man and I told you that he would never fight."

"Yes, I know you did, Laurie. But what made him go to town and pick a fight?"

"Someone made him do it. That is all I know in my heart."

"Tom," Bolt said, "I think we'd better go back to town. I don't think we got all the answers we were looking for."

The two men rode back into town and this time they ran into Phil Hodges, one of the regular customers at the Rocking Bar Bordello. Phil told them he had been an eyewitness to Ken's tragic death.

"You want to know why your pianner player got his lights blowed out?" Hodges asked.

"Yes. Do you know?" Bolt said.

"That Lew Badham called Laurette a whore and a degenerate, and a lot of other filthy things," Phil said.

"Then Ken was defending Laurette's honor," Bolt said, finally realizing why Ken challenged the man who killed him.

"Yeah," Phil said. "Badham called Selves a lot of names, too, but Selves said he didn't care about that. He wanted Badham to apologize for the dirty names he'd called Laurette in public."

"Did you see Ken take a drink at the Prairie Schooner?" Tom asked.

"No, but a friend of mine did. He said Selves told the bartender that he was takin' a farewell drink for Lew Badham."

"Hmmm," Bolt said. "Why would Badham insult Laurette, unless he wanted to put her out of business?"

"Maybe you'd better ask him that," Hodges said. "I'd say that one was after bigger fish to fry."

"What do you mean?" Bolt asked.

"Badham's a big gun up north, in Kansas, and ain't a one of the notches on his gun clean or fair. Badham's hired talent, Bolt, and he's done staked himself out a table at the Prairie Schooner."

Bolt thought about it as they rode back toward the ranch. They were almost home when he suddenly realized what was going on.

Lew Badham didn't kill Ken Selves just to put Laurette Armand out of business. Badham, a hired gun, wanted Bolt's hide.

And, behind Lew Badham's gun, was Monte Calhoun's money.

Bolt was sure of it.

"Tom, I gotta ride back into town," Bolt said as they turned into their place.

"Again?" Tom said.

"Yes. One more time and I think I'll have everything worked out. I want you to stay here with the girls."

Tom eyed Bolt suspiciously. "You know something you're not sharing with me," he said.

"Monte Calhoun hired Badham to kill me."

"You?"

"Yes. Calhoun was jealous of our whorehouse. You know he's always wanted one but the Women's Christian Society has always trampled his efforts to start one up in the city."

"But what about Ken?"

"Killing Ken was just a ruse to get me to face down Badham."

"And that's what you're planning to do. I don't like it, Bolt."

"It's got to be done, Tom."

"I'll go with you, then," Tom insisted.

"No, you stay here, and I don't want you to breathe a word of this to the girls. Not even if they beg you to tell them. And watch out for Laurette. That gal can be both stubborn and persuasive when she wants to be."

"Don't worry, Bolt, your secret's safe with me. Bolt?"

"Yeah?"

"Be careful."

"I will, Tom. Thanks."

Bolt stopped at the ranch only long enough to water his horse. Within minutes after he got to the ranch, he set out for town again.

Bolt's secret lasted exactly five minutes with Tom. Laurette had been standing at the window, gazing out at the bunkhouse where Ken had stayed, when Bolt watered his horse at the stable. She persuaded Tom to tell her where Bolt had gone.

"Tom, you've got to take Cherie and me to town," she said.

"I can't do it, Laurie," Tom said. "I promised Bolt."

"I don't care," Laurette cried. "I've got to stop him. I don't want Bolt's blood on my hands."

"Bolt doesn't want you there for what he's got to do."

"If you won't take us in the buggy, Cherie and I will ride to town on the horses."

Tom knew he'd just bought himself another trip to town. "Bolt won't like it," he said. "You'd better have a good reason to stop him."

"I do," Laurette said. "I love Bolt."

"I guess I can't argue with that." Tom grinned. "I'll bring the buggy around."

"I don't trust you, Tom. You'll stall until it's too late. Cherie and I are going with you to get the buggy. We've got to get there in time to stop Bolt."

"We're already too late," Tom said. "There's no way I can catch up to him now."

CHAPTER EIGHTEEN

The town was primed for a showdown by the time Bolt got there. He spotted the small crowd gathered near the Prairie Schooner as soon as he turned the corner onto the main road in San Antonio and, all along the street, curious bystanders looked his way.

Bolt tied his horse to the hitching post in front of the Alamo Hotel and checked both of his pistols again. Satisfied that they were ready if he needed them, he walked slowly along the creaking boardwalk, ignoring the bold stares of the people, ignoring their words of caution.

Several of the curious townsmen fell in behind him and then dropped back just before he reached the two-story building of the Prairie Schooner. The anxious crowd that had gathered in front of the saloon spread out when he got there, gave him room.

Bolt stepped off the boardwalk and took up a position in the street, some twenty feet away from the Prairie Schooner, directly in line with the batwing doors. He stood with his legs spread slightly, his arms loose by his sides, his hands hovering within easy reach of his holstered weapons.

"Badham!" Bolt shouted. "Lew Badham! Come out and fight like a man!"

Bolt saw the curtains part at the window. He saw someone look out briefly, but couldn't make out the face through the cloudy, smudged glass.

A minute later, the batwing doors swung open and a tall, dark-haired man with cruel eyes and a scarred face stepped through them. At the same instant, a buggy rattled up and stopped abruptly twenty-five feet from where Bolt stood, off to his right.

The buggy was almost in his line of vision and by shifting his eyes, he could see it. He was startled to see Tom in the driver's seat and Laurette and Cherie huddled next to him.

"Stop, Bolt!" Laurette cried out, her voice shaky and shrill with hysteria. "Don't do it, Bolt! You can't bring Ken back this way."

"Tom, take them away," Bolt ordered without taking his eyes off of Badham.

"Please, don't," Laurette called again. "Please, Jared Bolt, I love you. For my sake, don't do this thing."

Lew Badham swaggered out onto the boardwalk in front of the saloon, his arms held away from his body, his hands close to his guns. He laughed at Laurette's pleas.

"You gonna hide behind that French whore's skirts, Bolt?" he called.

Those were fighting words and Bolt knew there would be no talking Badham out of the showdown.

"You killed a better man than yourself, Badham," he said in a loud, even voice. "Ken Selves was a hero. He had some ideals, some character, which is something you know nothing about."

"You want to find out about my character?" Badham taunted, narrowing his eyes. "Go ahead and try it."

"You're nothing but a snake. Lower than that, even."

"So?"

"And, you have insulted a lady," Bolt said.

Lew Badham was cocky, sure of himself. He laughed again, louder this time. His harsh, cruel voice grated on Bolt's raw nerves like a sharp, jagged-edged saw blade.

"That Ken was as queer as a three-dollar bill," Badham yelled. "Maybe you are too, Bolt."

Tom Penrod, still sitting on the hard driver's seat, thought that Lew Badham was too confident. He glanced around. Something was not quite right. He rested his hand on the butt of his pistol.

Laurette and Cherie, both of them sensing that something was wrong, slowly slid away from Tom and huddled together on the far side of the seat. Both of them were near tears. Laurette was afraid to call out to Bolt again, fearful that she might distract him at the wrong time.

Bolt didn't notice the movement in the buggy. His attention was focused on the hired gunman.

"Badham, I'm gonna give you the same chance you gave Ken Selves," he said in a loud voice. "Make your move."

"First draw?"

"That's right."

Lew Badham was fast, smooth.

Bolt watched his eyes, not his flashing hands. Badham's eyes crinkled, narrowed to slits.

Bolt knew that was the instant of truth. His hand moved like a shadow, fast as a diving hawk. He cleared leather a split-second before Badham did. He thumbed back on the hammer as he raised his pistol. He didn't have to take aim. He knew his gun that well.

He fired and drilled Badham right in the heart.

Blood spurted from the hole in his chest, spread in a crimson blossom across the white shirt. Badham staggered back, gasped, clutched at his chest with his left hand, tried to bring his pistol to bear with his shooting hand.

Bolt shot him again.

The crowd cheered.

Badham jerked backwards, slammed against the batwing doors, then crumpled to the wooden slats of the boardwalk. He lay dead, his body in the doorway, the batwing doors swinging back and forth above him, the rusty hinges squeaking a death song as they slowed down and finally stopped.

A curtain in an upper-story window fluttered. The snout of a shotgun poked through, then aimed down at Bolt.

Bolt didn't see the movement at the high window. He didn't see the shiny metal of the barrel. He was looking down at Lew Badham.

"Look out!" someone on his left shouted.

A shot boomed out, the sound cracking the air. Bolt started to duck. He looked up and saw the shotgun at the window just as the barrel tilted upward and fired. Glass shattered with a loud crunching sound.

An instant later, Monte Calhoun pitched forward out of the high window, the side of his head a mass of blood and torn flesh. Calhoun's body dropped onto a sloped roof, then rolled off of that and crashed to the street with a loud, dull thud, just a few feet from where Bolt stood.

Bolt glanced around and saw the smoking pistol in Tom Penrod's hand. He walked over to the buggy.

"I owe you one, amigo," he said, the tension gradually easing from his shoulders.

"Not me," said Tom with a big grin. "You owe it to this little lady here," he said, nodding to Laurette. "If it hadn't been for her stubborn streak about coming to town, we wouldn't be here.'"

Bolt walked around to the other side of the buggy. He reached up and squeezed Laurette's hand. "Thank you, Laurie. I owe you one."

"I think I'll take you up on it." She smiled.

That evening, just after supper and while all of the girls were doing the dishes, Tom suggested to Bolt that they go out on the porch and leave the girls to their work.

"I'm going to spend the night in Cherie's cottage tonight," Tom said when they were outside.

"With her permission?" Bolt asked with a playful smile, even though he knew Tom and Cherie had already shared a bed before.

"Of course," Tom said, smiling.

"So why are you telling me?" Bolt asked. "I'm not really interested in your love life."

"You're really dumb, Bolt." Tom shook his head.

"Yeah," Bolt sighed. "I'm usually more careful than that."

"More careful than what?" Tom's face screwed up in puzzlement.

"I should have known Calhoun would be waiting in the shadows to blow me away. I should have checked my surroundings. I should have looked up." Bolt smiled. "I'm glad you were there, my friend."

"I am, too, Bolt, but that's not what I was talking about."

It was Bolt's turn to frown. "What in the hell are you getting at, Tom?" he said with a puzzled look. "You've lost me completely."

"I was trying to tell you that I'd be gone all night."

"So?"

"So, you'll have the house to yourself tonight. I hope you won't be lonely."

Bolt grinned. "Thanks, Tom. Maybe tonight will be the night."

Bolt shouldn't have had any doubts about it. Laurette came to his bed like a wanton hussy. She came with a need to get release from her grief, if only for a brief time. She came to Bolt's bed because she loved him, because she wanted him as desperately as he wanted her.

They made love more than once that night. The first time was full of wild passions and their twin needs to feel human again. The second time, just before dawn, was not as wild, but it was more satisfying to both of them. It was a time of freedom, when they could enjoy each other's company without the tension of the previous days.

"We'd better get up if you want to see the sunrise this morning," Bolt said much later. "It's already turning light." He slipped into trousers and a shirt while Laurie put her silk robe on.

Although they had no coffee that morning, they stood arm in arm in Bolt's living room and never said a word while they watched the dawn break on a brand-new day.

"Bolt, Cherie and I are going to leave today," Laurette said sadly after the red ball of sun broke the horizon.

"I thought you would," Bolt said. "Where are you going?"

"Back to New Orleans for a while, until I decide what I want to do with my life."

"You could stay here and sing if you wanted to."

"I couldn't do it. Bolt. Not without Ken here."

"I understand. Will you come back some day?" he asked.

"We just might. I love it here."

"I'll take you to town in the buggy whenever you're ready to go."

"I'd rather you didn't," Laurette said.

Bolt was surprised. He looked over at her and saw the tears in her eyes. "How will you get to town?"

"If it's all right with you, I'll ask Chet to take us."

"But . . ."

Laurette shook her head sadly.

"No, Bolt, I couldn't stand to say good-bye to you

at the stage stop."

"Yeah, partings are hard."

"They are when you love someone," Laurie said. "I love you, Bolt." Tears spilled over the brim of her eyes, trickled down her cheeks.

"I love you, too, Laurie," he said, close to tears himself.

"I wanted to say our good-byes with the beautiful sunrise. It will be a new day for both of us. A good day, I hope."

They kissed each other and then embraced for a long time as they gazed out at the pink clouds in the eastern sky.

"Whenever I see a sunrise, I'll think of you, Laurie," Bolt said.

"I'll do the same, Bolt. And don't forget the sunsets. I'll always remember my first night here when we shared the sunset. That's when I first fell in love with you."

"Well, I'll be damned," Bolt said. "I didn't know that."

"You weren't supposed to," Laurette said with a playful smile.

REACH FOR ZEBRA BOOKS
FOR THE HOTTEST IN ADULT WESTERN ACTION!

THE SCOUT
by Buck Gentry

16: VIRGIN OUTPOST	(1445, $2.50)
18: REDSKIN THRUST	(1592, $2.50)
19: BIG TOP SQUAW	(1699, $2.50)
20: BIG BAJA BOUNTY	(1813, $2.50)
21: WILDCAT WIDOW	(1851, $2.50)
22: RAILHEAD ROUND-UP	(1898, $2.50)
24: SIOUX SWORDSMAN	(2103, $2.50)
25: ROCKY MOUNTAIN BALL	(2149, $2.95)

Available wherever paperbacks are sold, or order direct from the publisher. Send cover price plus 50¢ per copy for mailing and handling to Zebra Books, Dept. 2387, 475 Park Avenue South, New York, N.Y. 10016. Residents of New York, New Jersey and Pennsylvania must include sales tax. DO NOT SEND CASH.

RIDE THE TRAIL TO RED-HOT ADULT WESTERN EXCITEMENT WITH ZEBRA'S HARD-RIDING, HARD-LOVING HERO...

SHELTER
by Paul Ledd

#18: TABOO TERRITORY	(1379, $2.25)
#19: THE HARD MEN	(1428, $2.25)
#22: FAST-DRAW FILLY	(1612, $2.25)
#23: WANTED WOMAN	(1680, $2.25)
#24: TONGUE-TIED TEXAN	(1794, $2.25)
#25: THE SLAVE QUEEN	(1869, $2.25)
#26: TREASURE CHEST	(1955, $2.25)
#27: HEAVENLY HANDS	(2023, $2.25)
#28: LAY OF THE LAND	(2148, $2.50)
#29: BANG-UP SHOWDOWN	(2240, $2.50)

Available wherever paperbacks are sold, or order direct from the Publisher. Send cover price plus 50¢ per copy for mailing and handling to Zebra Books, Dept. 2387, 475 Park Avenue South, New York, N.Y. 10016. Residents of New York, New Jersey and Pennsylvania must include sales tax. DO NOT SEND CASH.